A-M. V. Geos

CW00868186

Inside or Out

by Onia Fox

(Jessica Taylor series book four)

Also by Onia Fox

Covid Blues and Twos – erotic drama

Listless in Turkey – travel thriller (Jessica Taylor series book one)

Enemy Close – procedural suspense thriller (Jessica Taylor series book two)

Connecting Doors – locked room murder mystery (Jessica Taylor series book three)

Ras Putin – Prince of Russia – comedy parody

sauce for the goose

Jessica Taylor returns home just in time for Christmas, following a scrape with the Indian Police Service and the scrutiny of British Special Branch. She has no secrets from her husband and, one day when the time is right, she will tell him about her Indian dalliances. She wonders when, or if, the time will ever be right.

First, she needs to fix her marriage to the man she loves more than life itself. She returns home to find a pair of women's shoes, a silk scarf, and then a half-naked young woman in her house. She makes one reckless mistake too many.

Dedicated to my gorgeous wife and soulmate:

She never did like my hero, Jessica Taylor

Inside or Out

Contents

Chapter One 1

Chapter Two 6

Chapter Three 22

Chapter Four 41

Chapter Five 50

Chapter Six 65

Chapter Seven 81

Chapter Eight 95

Chapter Nine 122

Chapter Ten 144

Chapter Eleven 159

Chapter Twelve 179

Chapter Thirteen 189

Chapter Fourteen 192

Chapter Fifteen 195

Chapter One

Jessica lay back on her fully reclined Singapore Airlines business class seat. She boarded the flight a little tipsy on brandy and champagne from the party but had the sense to slip on her silk pyjamas under the business suit. Having packed her own cabin bag before the party, housekeeping then packed her hold luggage, before pouring her towards the terminal, with the help of security and an electric buggy.

Jessica crashed the British Airways flight crew's stopover party, thankfully not the same crew flying her home today. She was the centre of attention - fresh blood - but did not stray as she had on her first night in India. The most flirtatious of the crew was not really her type – attractive enough, funny, attentive, but too … female.

With a slightly spinning head, Jessica planned her reunion with Jason. There was still work to do in their marriage. He knew her contract in India was complete but did not know she was on this flight, or even if she would make it home for Christmas day. If she could sneak past, or pacify Brian, her dog, she would creep up to the bedroom and whisper to Jason through the door. Better not risk receiving a knuckle sandwich by leaping on him from the dark. She listened to *The Author* by Luz on her noise cancelling earphones. Perhaps she would sing to him through the door.

The couple had no secrets, but she might not tell Jason everything that happened in India straight away. She decided to wait until the time was right. Perhaps the time would never be right, but that was not the same as actual lying. However she looked at it, the airline pilot on the first night and her junior project engineer over the past fortnight was, technically, still cheating – despite the distance. As she drifted asleep, she remembered the eagerness of her junior colleague to please.

Showered on the flight and wearing red skinny jeans, with a thick, black cable knit boyfriend-jumper and boots against the English winter, Jessica walked through arrivals with her luggage and onto the main Heathrow concourse. She expected to see her name on a taxi driver's board, but instead saw a beaming, familiar face. She abandoned her case, her coat falling to the floor, and ran to the man, throwing her arms around his neck and burying her face in his chest.

'Parker! What are you doing out at two in the morning? God, it's good to see you.'

Laughing, the driver tried to ease Jessica away from his chest, but she redoubled her clench, rubbing her nose and face against his shirt. She inhaled the faint smoky odour from an open fire, Persil washing powder, and starch.

'You smell of home, Parker. Thank you for coming to get me. Shit, I've got lipstick on your shirt!'

Parker eased her away this time, still laughing.

'Mrs Parker knows it is you I am collecting. The worst I will receive is a tut. Let's find your bag before security blow it up. I took the shout from your PA and took the job myself. I can't trust just anyone with my favourite Mrs Taylor. How was India?'

Parker parked the company limo at the top of the steps to Jessica's close. He carried the cases to outside her front door, Jessica gesturing with a silencing finger to her lips. She could not tip her friend, but she would find a suitable gift to give him in work from the pile she brought back for Jason. Recognising Jessica's turn of the key, Brian did not bark. But he twisted and bucked across the floor in greeting, torn between jumping over his mistress and finding a toy to show her. Stifling a giggle, she stroked and petted him until he calmed, offering him the dog-chew she kept ready in her pocket. Jessica stretched from her journey, removed her boots, and saw the pair of women's shoes discarded near the front door. On the leather chair lay a silk scarf. Her heart pounded. She wanted to run after Parker and climb back into the safety of his backseat. A door opened from upstairs.

'Brian! You are joking. You've been out already, Jeez!'

Jessica climbed the stairs as Jason descended, wearing just shorties.

'Jace.'

'Jessica! Oh my God, you startled me! Wow! You're home. Wait, wait for me.'

Jessica ducked under his open arms and pushed past to the narrow corridor leading to their, *her,* bedroom. She kicked open the door to an empty room.

'Right Jess, you need to ease off and listen for a moment.'

She spun around to face her husband, his hands raised, palms facing out to placate his wife. The guest room door, at the opposite end of the corridor and back near the top of the stairs, opened. Framed in the doorway stood a young woman wearing Jason's Dennis the Menace and Gnasher T-shirt.

'Mrs Taylor! Jessica. Jess.'

Jessica strode at her husband. He walked backwards slowly, giving his wife time to calm, without physically blocking her. Jessica stopped, took a deep breath, and looked at her feet. Jason relaxed, dropping his hands to his sides.

'Ok. Now, listen to me carefully, love.'

Jessica slowly raised her face to make eye contact with her husband before head-butting him on the bridge of his nose. He fell backwards, cracking the back of his head against the threshold to the guestroom. Jessica stepped forward, stamping down hard on Jason's groin. She found her balance and stamped on his solar plexus. Priti took a step backwards, backing against the Welsh dresser. Jessica took another step forward, standing on Jason's chest as he struggled to stand, gripping Jessica's ankle.

Jessica grabbed Priti's hair and pulled back her fist. Priti moved both her hands in front of her belly for

4

protection. Jessica let go the punch just as Jason stood, still gripping her ankle. Unbalanced, the punch was weak, but still contacted Priti's chin. As Jessica fell forward, she gripped Priti's hair with both hands. Jason picked her off the floor by her waist. Still gripping Priti's hair, the women's faces pushed together. Finding Priti's nose, she bit hard, feeling the gristle bubble, and burst in her mouth. Priti screamed with pain as Jessica's mouth filled with blood.

Jason used his free hand to pull back Jessica's head by her hair. Taller, broader, and stronger than Jessica, Jason continued to restrain his wife by the hair and around her waist.

'Darling! Nothing …'

Jessica brought back her elbow into Jason's open jaw, breaking the bone and dislocating the joint. Jason stumbled backwards, refusing to release his wife to further injure Priti. Using Jason's grip, Jessica brought up both feet and kicked out at Priti. One foot contacted Priti's belly as the other slammed into her cheek. Jason and Jessica fell back into the corridor. Using his greater strength, Jason rolled on top of his wife. He tried to punch the side of her head, but she was more agile and folded her head under his chest.

Barely able to speak with a shattered cheek, Priti dialled 999.

'*Emergency services. Which service do you require?*'

Chapter Two

'My client has prepared a written statement, which I shall submit to you. It reads:

'I returned home following a long journey. I was tired. I walked to my bedroom but was confronted by an intruder. I defended myself from attack until my husband restrained me and explained we had a guest staying. I have nothing further to add at this stage.

'I have offered my client legal advice, suggesting she makes no further comment. Unless you have compelling evidence to the contrary, to disclose, I request you release my client.'

The police inspector snorted.

'Sorry inspector? You find this funny?'

'Where to start, Mrs Wilson, where to start?'

The detective sergeant spoke. 'Mrs Taylor. You are still under caution and have your legal representative present. Mrs Taylor, you seriously assaulted your friend and colleague, Priti Khan.'

'No friend of mine.'

'I have just informed you …'

'Mrs Wilson!' The inspector interjected. 'You will remain silent, as in *shut up*, during this interview!'

Jessica's brief laid a hand on Jessica's forearm.

'No comment.'

'And attacked your own husband as he defended Ms Khan and himself.'

'No comment. Is my dog ok?'

'No comment, Mrs Taylor,' offered the inspector. The sergeant continued.

'Do you suspect your husband and Ms Khan were having an affair? Is that why you tried to kill her?'

'Kill her!' Jessica and her brief shouted in unison.

'Mrs Wilson…'

'Don't Mrs Wilson me inspector! You have cautioned my client investigating an assault. Has something changed?'

'Mrs Taylor…'

'Is my dog ok?'

'Quid pro quo, Mrs Taylor?'

'Tu primus, sergeant.'

'Your dog attacked our officer. Our officers defended themselves by kicking your dog until it ceased to attack them. Fortunately, a dog unit was in attendance who administered *doggy* first aid and took it to *doggy* hospital. It has broken ribs and a punctured lung, but is likely to recover. Your reason to viciously attack your husband and *friend*?'

'She is always all over him. Our relationship is so special, but he is only human. She waited until I was away. Jason is everything to me. She has taken that from me.'

'So, you tried to kill her?'

Mrs Wilson moved to object again, but Jessica continued.

'I was not thinking of anything. She was there, barely covering her pussy in my husband's T-shirt. He

7

was wearing even less. They provoked me. I lashed out.'

'Repeatedly?'

'No comment.'

'It doesn't work like that, Mrs Taylor.'

'I need to see my husband.'

'No chance. He is both a victim and a witness.'

'He won't press charges against me.'

'It is us, the police, prosecuting this case, Mrs Taylor.'

'Look, the slut was in my house. I slapped her. Move on.'

'And was he? Did he tell you he was?'

'Was what?'

'Fucking your friend?'

'She is his friend, not mine.'

'Mrs Taylor?'

'No. But it was kind of obvious.'

'Mrs Wilson, Mrs Taylor,' the inspector spoke again. 'We are not looking to offer police bail. We will look to extend your questioning and ask the courts to keep you on remand. We suspect you are a flight risk – with connections to India, Syrian Kurdistan, and property in Turkey.'

'Bloody hell Jess!'

'Don't swear at me Jackie.'

'All this other shit! This is not a game, Jess. They are looking to move this to attempted murder. No more bollocks!'

'I own a beach shack in Turkey. I have no connections to Kurds in Syria, at least none living. I travel a bit for work. My grandad was half Afghani or something. I visited once as a kiddie, but I was born here, in England. I have nowhere to *flight to.*'

'Christ! And would you have stopped? Stopped kicking her to death? Don't answer that, I am an officer of the court. I don't want to know. What do you know they know? What is going on?'

'I have no idea, Jackie. Ask them. Isn't it disclosure or something? Ask the filth, not me.'

'They won't disclose anything during their investigation. The CPS will disclose the evidence once they have a case to prosecute. Until then, you need to sing to your brief, or they can't help you.'

'My brief? You are my brief.'

'I'm here to represent you during interview. I am prepared to continue representing you until you are bailed, released, or charged. But if this becomes attempted murder, you need to look at hiring a firm slightly more *dedicated.* I do volume crime at barely minimum wage.

'What happens now?'

'You didn't even ask how your victims are.'

'I don't care. They deserve it.'

'Have you never slept with a married man, Jess?'

'Not in his wife's house!'

'Oh, that's ok, then. And what happened to a statement and going *no comment*? Whose side are you on, Jess?'

'Look Jackie, I obviously slapped the bitch. Can't I just plead guilty to assault, pay for her nose job, and move on with my fucked-up marriage?'

'If they charge you with a crime, which you are guilty of, I will, of course, advise you to plead guilty. I will try to mitigate the sentence, but you will have a criminal record and can say goodbye to a career working for a security company, which contracts to the government.'

'I couldn't care less. I'll jack it in. I want to look at doing fostering, anyway.'

'Fostering! No chance. Not with a *crim.*'

'It's our dream. Jason and I have plans.'

Mrs Wilson scoffed at Jessica's reply, then softened when she saw her eyes well.

'One step at a time, Jess. You've blown the *no comment* option. Juries don't like defendants pick 'n mixing. You can't just choose to answer the question you like the sound of.'

'Jury? For assaulting a slut fucking my husband?'

'Let's see what they come up with. We go back in and continue with the intruder angle. If, when, they drill down, say you were anxious about an intruder in the house. Then, when you saw her in bed with your husband…'

'They weren't actually in bed together. He was on the stairs. She was in the spare room.'

'You saw him first? So, you were not really worried about an intruder?' Jessica shrugged. 'But you had reasons to think he had got out of her bed?'

Jessica shrugged again. 'She hadn't come round to mow the lawn.'

'Lose the attitude, Jessica. You are in enough trouble. A nod means answer, carefully. A shake means don't answer.'

'You heard a noise upstairs. Probably your husband. What made you so anxious?'

Mrs Wilson nodded.

'I thought someone else was in the house.'

'Why did you think that?'

'I just had a feeling.'

The sergeant studied a sheet of paper from his folder.

'Nothing more tangible? A pair of shoes in the front room, perhaps.' Jessica nodded. 'For the tape, Mrs Taylor.'

'Yes, I saw a pair of shoes.'

'Male or female?'

'I didn't notice.'

'Colour?'

'Red, I think.'

'Style?'

'Not sure. Low heel perhaps. Patent, maybe.'

'Not your husband's usual footwear?' Jessica ignored the question. 'Anything else?'

Jessica sighed. 'A silk scarf.'

'Female's?'

'Yes! Yes, I thought Jason had a woman upstairs.'

'And you went upstairs to attack her.'

'No. I went upstairs to see who it was.'

'You did not know it might be your family friend, Priti Khan?'

'Priti works for the same company as me. Jason sometimes contracts to Company and the three of us worked together. She is no friend of mine, and she wrecked his marriage. She is young enough to be his daughter, for Christ's sake!'

'But you never suspected they might have had an affair? You did not go upstairs expecting to confront Priti Khan?'

'No. Absolutely not. I trust my husband with her. Trusted.'

'Mrs Taylor. Did you ever confide to your husband that you hacked Priti Khan's personal photograph file on her work laptop and found photos of your husband? Photographs which you believed to be inappropriately numerous and affectionate by nature?'

Mrs Wilson stopped nodding and shaking and now just stared at Jessica. Jessica shrugged.

'I know I can be impetuous sometimes. Answer me something, sergeant. Would you not lash out at someone who had been trying to get your partner into bed? And succeeded.'

The inspector interjected. 'We ask the questions, Mrs Taylor.'

'You think it acceptable to injure, badly, two people under such circumstances?' continued the sergeant.

Mrs Wilson shook her head. 'Gentlemen, you are not investigating my client's moral compass or her understanding of the law regarding provocation. I am struggling to understand where you are going with this. Mrs Taylor has admitted she lashed out under provocation, which I suspect any court will appreciate. Can we not give my client the counselling you might feel she deserves and allow these people to piece back together their lives?'

Neither officer shifted their gaze from Jessica. The inspector continued.

'Are you pro-life or pro-abortion, Mrs Taylor?'

'Don't answer that, Jess! You listen here…'

'No Mrs Wilson, you listen! One more outburst and I will have you removed. Your client may choose to answer anyway she wishes, and with your advice. But you, Mrs Wilson, will stay quiet. Perhaps your client will be better served by a lawyer who knows the law!'

'I can't answer that. It is a ridiculous question and totally unfairly loaded. Nobody is *pro-abortion*. No girl or woman looks forward to the day she can have an abortion. I am pro-choice, yes, but there is no such thing as *pro-abortion*.'

'Did you choose not to have children, Mrs Taylor? Another *choice*? And a choice your husband concurs with?'

'I am answering no more questions about my choices or otherwise regarding children. I cannot think a court will think badly of me. This is a disgusting line of questioning.'

'Where do you go to discuss such things, Mrs Taylor?'

'I have never had …' Mrs Wilson laid a silencing hand on Jessica's forearm.

'If you had a falling out with your husband, as we now know can happen, with serious consequences, where do you go? To whom? When you need advice, counselling, or a sympathetic ear, where do you go? Your mother? Sister?' Jessica scoffed. The sergeant studied the same sheet of paper. 'Your husband gave me a name.'

Jessica raised her face, making deliberate eye contact with the sergeant.

'My best friend is Amara Pebbles. I obviously have not discussed this situation with her.'

'But she knows you suspect Priti Khan has designs on your husband? Did she agree with your concerns?'

'She thought I was barking up the wrong tree.'

'How do you know Amara Pebbles?'

'God, this is boring. You are boring. Am is a colleague. She was my unofficial mentor, and we became close in and out of work. Alpha males dominate the arms industry, Amara has supported several young women in their early days. So what?'

'She mentored Priti Khan?'

'No. Different departments.'

'Who mentored Priti Khan?'

'No idea. Ask her.'

'We have Mrs Taylor. We have already. Now we are asking you.'

'You mean me? Priti oversaw a contract, to which Jason sub-contracted. I was on a different job, but the three of us were based in Turkey, together. I kept an eye on things and advised her on the project management side. She is bright and capable. With my guidance, Jason's and her job went very well. It makes me nauseous saying their names together, in the same breath.'

'When you weren't hacking her photos.'

'You are so hilarious.'

'You said Priti Khan is like a daughter to you and your husband. Where would…'

'No! I did not say that! I was just saying Jason is older than her. Her desire for him sexually is totally inappropriate. I am only a few years older than her – she is like no daughter of mine.'

'Jason is older than you also, Mrs Taylor. But that is less inappropriate?'

'Oh, for God's sake! He is nearly ten years older than I am. I am ten years older than his little slut. He might like her enormous eyes, tiny tits, and dilated pupils, but she does nothing for me!'

'Gentlemen, please. We need a comfort break. I, for one, need the loo and a cuppa. I need a brief word with my client.'

The police officer remained outside the toilet. Mrs Wilson headed straight for the cubical. Jessica leant against the open doorframe, staring up at a broken frosted window as sleet and snow lashed against it.

'What are they prattling on about, Jackie? Priti, Jason, and I have no kids between us. This is nothing to do with children. I have two nieces, but I haven't seen them since going to India. Jason has, but my sister and brother-in-law would have been there. If Jason has introduced Priti to my nieces, I'll finish them both off, and happily swing for it.'

'They are building a case, Jessica. To prove attempted murder, there needs to be some premeditation. Or at least the use of a weapon – please tell me there was no weapon. Used, threatened, or inferred?'

'God no. The little tart was a pushover; there is nothing of her. I didn't need a weapon.'

'Don't let them rile you, Jess. Answer truthfully, but offer nothing they don't specifically ask. Don't answer vague or general questions. Let them hang without a response. Make them ask more specific questions – where, why, when, and who.'

'You were about to tell me where this young woman might come for advice, sympathy, or protection.'

'Protection? From what?'

'Mrs Taylor?'

'I have no idea. Ask her.'

'But she came to you before?'

'We worked together. I am more senior and experienced.'

'But she wouldn't go to Jason?'

'Possibly. He is very supportive of her. I mean at work, not just when she is riding him like a cowgirl.'

'But she never came to you for emotional help outside of work?'

'We were working in the east of Turkey. There was a frightening military experience. We all stuck together.'

'So, she did come to you?'

'Your words.'

'And all this time you were preparing to defend your territory.'

'Yes, why not? I would do anything to keep my husband.'

'Sorry gentlemen. Before you move on, may I ask you to clarify and ask my client that question again, please?'

'Mrs Taylor, you threatened to stab your husband with rusty kitchen scissors for having an affair with Priti Khan. What had you planned for Priti, herself?'

'No! That is not what I said. And Jason would not have told you that. You have twisted his words. I saw how she looked at him. I was managing his awareness of the situation. It was a joke.'

'Joke? You are so hilarious, Mrs Taylor. Sometime ago, you chose a weapon to use against your husband and Priti Khan, for when the situation arose. A weapon which would always be to hand.'

'Rubbish! There was no weapon. She stood there, all pussy and legs. I whacked her. I had nothing in my hand, not even a tissue. I could have got a knife from the kitchen, but I didn't!'

'You could have got a knife? You felt capable of using a knife?'

'No! I meant there was an opportunity to find a weapon. But I did not want to use a weapon. Stop twisting everything I say.'

'You did not use a weapon? You did not premeditate the use of a weapon?'

'No! Absolutely not!'

The sergeant lay photographs of bruised and battered Jason and Priti on the desk and studied a separate sheet of paper.

'A big lad, Jason. Works in construction, runs, works out. Tall, broad, quite the hunk.'

Jessica glanced at the photos and away, bringing her hand to her mouth.

'Interested in how they are doing, Mrs Taylor? You haven't asked.'

'I thought you asked the questions. How are they recovering, please?'

'You asked about your dog. Anyway. Life changing, as you ask. Let's have a look.' The sergeant read from the A4 sheet.

'Taylor: Broken jaw, dislocated jaw. Broken nose, fractured eye socket. Concussion. Hydrocele to the left testicle. Fractured rib to right side, fractured sternum. Dislocated jaw and fractured jawbone requiring emergency operation to stabilise, wires fitted. Ouch!' Jessica sobbed. 'Khan: hair and scalp damage to both sides. Partially severed nose requiring immediate reconstructive and grafting operation to save the organ. Fractured cheek requiring emergency operation to stabilise, plate fitted. Bruising to lower abdomen. Bruising and impact shock to internal organs, including uterus. Emergency induced coma to protect …'

'Ok. Please, enough.'

The sergeant flicked between two paragraphs, comparing the entries in his mind. 'Here we go: likely causes - stamping, kicking, elbow punch, fist punch, head butt, drop kick, pushing, pulling. Tasty Mrs Taylor. Tasty.

'Let me ask again, Mrs Taylor. Did you use a weapon?'

Jessica answered, her voice shaking, tears streaming down her face. 'Let me answer again, sergeant. I used no weapon.'

He sat back in his chair and closed the folder on the desk. 'How do you stay fit, Mrs Taylor? Any sports?'

'I run, mostly. I used to play football, now I play a little five-a-side. I kickbox.'

'Kickbox, Mrs Taylor? Any belts?'

Mrs Wilson sat upright, turning to stare at Jessica.

'Yes, sergeant. I am a green belt.'

Mrs Wilson released an audible groan. The two police officers smiled.

'Let's leave it there for the moment.'

'Jess, using your learnt, practiced, assessed, and recognised skills as a kickboxer is totally the use of a weapon. You had a weapon to attack your victims,

19

which they did not possess to defend themselves. There are two constituents of an attempted murder, which the CPS and the courts will look for regarding culpability. Premeditation and the use of a weapon. And regarding the *harm* aspect, they will look for serious and/or permanent harm to the victim. Your kickboxing skill is the weapon. You suspected Priti of trying to seduce your husband and had warned off Jason previously – that will sound like premeditation. The injuries are permanent. Psychologically and physically, especially with permanent plates, hydrocele mesh fitted, and plastic surgery.'

'I did not attempt to murder anyone. I was provoked.'

'I disagree, and so will the courts. Neither victim admitted nor suggested they were having an affair. Priti may have come to your house for help or advice, as you say she has before. And provocation might mitigate a common assault sentence, but hardly justifies attempted murder! You told me if Jason has introduced Priti to your family, then you will kill them and take the consequence. Another joke?'

'She may have just been visiting? And then all her clothes fell off? Come on, Jackie.'

'You might never know now, Jess. Because you beat and pummelled two healthy adults before bothering to take a moment to ask.'

'Jackie, there is something else.'

'Here we go.'

'I am just about holding it together in cells. I can't go to prison.'

'You won't have a choice.'

'For how long?'

'One step at a time, Jess. You aren't charged yet.'

'Please. I need to get my head around this.'

'I will fight for bail and keep fighting, but if they charge you with attempted murder and if bail is denied, you are looking at months on remand before trial. Think maybe one year.'

'A year! Shit. Then what?'

'If the court takes the worst view, as I suggested a moment ago, you are looking at a nominal sentence of around twenty-years – with a *harm category* 2 and with medium culpability. The best I am hoping for at the moment is GBH without revenge at five-years. But with the ferocity of the attack and possible premeditation, we are fighting a six to ten-year stretch, even for GBH. I would like to suggest you will be out early with good behaviour – but from what I have seen of your behaviour so far, I am not so sure.'

Chapter Three

'Mrs Taylor. Please follow me.'

'Not again! I need some sleep.'

'You were sleeping? I thought you were rocking on your bunk. Come on, please.' Jessica followed the uniform back to the interview room.

'Where is my brief?'

'Hello Mrs Taylor, good to meet you. I am DC Williamson.'

Jessica studied the badge.

'Adolphus! What sort of name is that?'

The DC scoffed. 'My friends call me Dolly.'

'Where is my brief?'

'This is just a quick chat, Mrs Taylor. No need for an audience. Nothing you say to me is *admiss*. I won't keep you long.'

'A Detective Sergeant and a Detective Inspector have interviewed me. Why am I now talking to a Detective Constable? Scraping the barrel? Or is this just a sleep deprivation technique?'

The DC scoffed again. 'Hardly, Mrs Taylor. We were having a flick through your file. You've been busy.'

'Who is *we*?'

'A run in with the Indians and previously with the Turks and Kurds in Syria.'

'What do you want, DC Dolly?'

'Are you Muslim, Mrs Taylor, nee Khan?'

'No! And mind your own business!'

'Never mind. I assume you are not related to the poor creature you broke?'

'Khan is my maiden name. It is quite common. I am no relation to Priti. No more questions without my brief.'

'We can't decide if you are fearless, or stupid, Miss Khan.'

'*We* who? Stupid. Now fuck off and let me go back to my cell.'

'You must be dreading a twenty-year stretch, especially with the baby thing. You won't be popular inside.'

'What *baby* thing?'

'Even this police custody stint must seem arduous for such a free spirit.'

'What *baby* thing?'

'I had a few ideas for helping you out of this predicament, Miss Khan. But you do *stupid* very well.'

'What sort of *help*?'

'I don't know Miss Khan…'

'Taylor!'

'… you say. What would make you feel a little better? Some fags? Chocolates? Less dowdy tracksuit? Decent shower? Bail and a meeting with your husband?'

'Your DI said he would oppose bail and Jason is off limits.'

'Ok. How about just the tracksuit and shower?'

'There was a terrible misunderstanding. I need to talk with Jason.'

'Sure. I will see what I can do.'

'Why?'

'As you ask, Miss Khan, I could do with some assistance.'

'To do what?'

'Oh, you know. This and that.'

'You are a bit of a wanker, DC Dolly.'

The DC scoffed for the third time.

'We are interested in your involvement with the international security industry, your Muslim background, and your approach to life generally.'

'Who the fuck are you, DC Dolly? And I have no Muslim heritage.'

'We have a little influence over police investigations. We have less influence over the CPS, especially once they have your file for prosecution. We have no influence over the courts.'

'And *we* is *who*?'

'But wow, wouldn't it be cool if you had a nice Christmas with your friends and came back in the new year for a suspended sentence or even just a caution?'

'And you can do that?'

'No, Miss Khan. But you can. You must be anxious about your dual nationality. We deport convicted dual nationals.'

'I don't have dual nationality! I am English! British! A UK citizen. You need to flick slower through my file, dickhead.'

The DC slowly and deliberately took a twenty-pound note from his wallet, sliding it across the table to Jessica.

'A present Miss Khan.'

'I earn more in a week than you do in a month, officer.'

'Who is that?'

'The Queen. So?'

'No, it isn't. The Queen is dead; doesn't exist.'

'It is still the Queen. Long live the King.'

'How much is it worth?'

'Twenty pounds.'

'No, it isn't. What does that say?'

'*I promise to pay the bearer the sum of twenty pounds.*'

'And what does twenty pounds look like, Miss Khan? If you went to Threadneedle Street to have it paid.'

'No idea. A bit of gold, perhaps. Probably not very much gold.'

'The gold standard went many years ago, Miss Khan.'

'You have lost me.'

'It is only your Queen because it says it is. It is only worth twenty pounds because it says it is. It is a game we all play. You are a dual Afghan national and will be deported at the end of your prison sentence, because I have a piece of paper to say you are.

'You have nominated two addresses to be released to, on bail. Your sister is out of the question because of the baby thing, and she has two children at that address. But the Guildford address of your friend Amara Pebbles looks more promising, despite being out of county. Or I hear Kingston Prison in Portsmouth is having a turkey roll for Christmas lunch. I am sure you will make the most of the day wherever you are.'

'What *baby thing*?'

'Jess. We need to lean on the DI today. Your twenty-four hours are up, and he needs to charge you, release you, release you on bail, or release you under further investigation.'

'He hinted at extending questioning by twelve hours, Jax.'

'That worries me a little, which is why I need to force his hand. He has questioned you about the assault and you have answered his questions. He cannot just hold you whilst repeating the same questions. But he can ask the magistrate to hold you on remand for a few weeks, or until your initial court date. This is serious, Jess, but you have not absconded before. I don't think the magistrate will remand, especially as you remain un-charged.'

'Good. Home for Christmas.'

'I think he will ask the Superintendent to extend questioning. If he gets another twelve hours, that will put you past 5pm on Christmas eve. If he then opposes bail, you will be kept in custody until after Christmas. I can push and push for a hearing bank holiday 26th December, but my guess is you will be lucky to find a magistrate before the 27th or even the first working day, which is 28th December.'

'You just said he had to have some new line of questioning.'

'You are good at seeing your life through *Jessica* tinted spectacles. I am going to ask you again. Is there anything else that happened during the attack, or the build-up, which you haven't told me about?'

'There was no build-up!'

The couple sat in silence with Mrs Wilson not prepared to allow Jessica to sidestep the question. Jessica ran over the illicit meeting with DC Dolly in her head – not yet prepared to divulge and slam shut that door, by reporting the incident to Mrs Wilson.

'I bumped into a police officer, early hours. They said something odd.'

'You *bumped* into a police officer! Where, who? Whilst out for a stroll?'

'I don't remember. Maybe outside my cell. Look, he said something strange.'

'Did he give a name?'

'Not that I remember.'

'Shit Jess! What did he say?'

'He mentioned a baby.'

'What baby? In what context?'

Jessica shrugged. 'The filth said something odd yesterday as well.'

'This whole thing is odd, Jessica. What part sticks out in your mind?'

'They said the hospital put Priti into an induced coma. For a sore cheek? I don't think so.'

'Mrs Taylor, I remind you, you are still under caution.'

'DI, before you continue, I would like to voice a concern on behalf of my client. You will realise my client has been under arrest for just over twenty-four hours without charge.'

'I was about…'

'And before you announce your intention to request a twelve-hour extension to questioning, I have a proposal for you. You see, Detective Inspector, your filibustering until the magistrates have headed home for the break is hardly complying to the spirit of the Police and Criminal Evidence Act, and not to the word of the Policing and Crime Act. Now that I have pointed this out to you and have a proposal to avoid this miscarriage, it will be inappropriate for you to further follow this path. My practice has already contacted your superintendent to discuss, prior to her offering the extension I suspect you are about to ask for.'

'Mrs Wilson, it is absolutely within my remit to ask a superintendent…'

'Whereas my proposal will give you access to my client before you feel the need to twist the rules. Or am I to report, at 0800 hrs on this Saturday morning, you have a plan to keep my client in custody for 96 hours without the scrutiny of a magistrate?'

'Mrs Wilson, I have every authority…'

'Sorry DI. Is that a no? You will not explore my proposal?'

The DS sat back, flicking glances between his senior officer and Mrs Wilson. The DI turned an angry red.

'Go on, Mrs Wilson. Propose away.'

'You release my client from custody, as of now – over 24 hours following her arrest. My client will volunteer to remain here to answer your questions about this mysterious third charge. If your questioning is not complete by noon, we walk out of here and home. Or we all go in front of the magistrate together – as per PACE.'

'We do not have any mysterious lines of questioning, Mrs Wilson. And I am not delaying.'

'Good, DI. Let's get cracking. My client has Christmas presents to buy.'

The DI nodded to his Detective Sergeant.

'Mrs Taylor, I want to clarify a couple…'

'Sorry to interrupt again, DS. Let's cut the crap. Let's get to the point and waste no more time. Eh, Sergeant? The baby. You want to ask about the baby. Only this line of enquiry around the baby is new and will gain you an extension from your *super*. Let's all focus.'

The DS glanced at his DI again, who nodded back.

'Mrs Taylor. What do you know about the baby?'

'I know nothing about any baby.'

The DS fumbled through his folder. He could not decide if she knew or did not know. If he had the advantage of surprise, or if she was about to confess to premeditated infanticide. He cleared his throat.

'Mrs Taylor. Why did you kick Priti Khan in the lower abdomen?'

Both women looked incredulously at the question. The DI closed his eyes for a moment, the DS blushed.

'Where have you been this past twenty-four hours, sergeant? I kicked the slut because she is fucking my husband. Wakey-wakey, keep up.'

'And you knew she was pregnant, before you tried to kill Priti Khan and her unborn child?'

Jessica stood, wide eyed, both hands to her face.

'Sit down, Mrs Taylor.'

Jessica took a step backwards, away from the men. Her chair upended and, before Mrs Wilson could grab her, Jessica tripped, falling into the tangle of chair legs. The DS pushed the alarm, and a uniform entered. Both detectives and Mrs Wilson were at Jessica's side to help her stand. Only when Jessica was back on her feet, leaning against the DS, and the uniform had righted the chair for Jessica to sit, did Jessica let out a scream and buckle.

Jessica managed some toast and coffee. The custody sergeant accepted Jessica's assurance she had lost her balance following hearing the accusation and required no medical intervention. Jessica sat back in the interview room, waiting for the decision regarding police bail and the alternatives.

'To be frank, Mrs Wilson, I am leaning towards requesting your client is remanded in custody.'

'You know, and I know, DI, that any magistrate will not buy into your flight risk concerns. You have not charged Mrs Taylor, and she has no criminal history, let alone any for absconding. She has fully cooperated regarding the alleged assault, and the CPS won't take your attempted murder allegation seriously, let alone infanticide! Infanticide? Come on DI.'

The DI's phone pinged a message. He subconsciously turned to face the mirror and camera behind him before reading the message.

'I have some questions about my arrest, please.'

'Go on, Mrs Taylor.'

'Why is a DI, and a DS, involved in this relatively low-level crime of assault?'

'We are investigating a possible attempted murder and infanticide Mrs Taylor. It is up to us and the superintendent as to the allocation of police personnel and resource to a case.'

'And also, since when has a Detective Constable sat behind a one-way mirror issuing instructions to a more senior inspector, Inspector?'

The DI turned an angry red again.

'You may ask questions about your own arrest, Mrs Taylor, but not about our operational procedures.' The DI's phone pinged again. 'Mrs Taylor, Mrs Wilson. Thank you for staying behind and voluntarily assisting with our enquiries past the twenty-four hours custodial period. I have decided not to ask for a further extension for questioning and will not look to apply for magistrates to detain you on remand. I will release you on police bail to appear in front of the magistrate or back here at a future date. You will have strict bail conditions applied. I am sure Mrs Wilson will talk you through the process.'

Mrs Wilson eased her car along the A3 towards Guildford. The outside lane was closed by snow, the inside lane congested, but the middle lane moved at forty miles per hour over freezing slush.

'You know how the law applies to everyone, except Jessica Taylor?'

'Don't start Jackie. I am paying your wages. If you have something to say, just say it.'

'The taxpayer is technically paying my wages, Jess.'

'Yes, about that. I want to instruct you to act for me until this is resolved. I need a brief who has witnessed the pig's strange and heavy-handed behaviour. I don't want to start with a rookie who, you know.'

'Know what?'

'I want you. You stand up to me.'

'I will have my office prepare a schedule of costs. Even we don't come cheap when privately instructed – but we are probably cheaper than many.'

'Whatever. I have some savings. I am not looking to leave them invested and untouched for twenty-years. Anyway, you were about to kick me whilst I am down.'

'Answer these questions calmly. I am trying not to get us squashed in a motorway pile-up here. Did you know, or even suspect, Priti was pregnant?'

'No! Of course not. I am not a monster.'

'Could you see a bump?'

Jessica shuddered. 'I could see what she had for breakfast. There was no bump.'

'So, she was less than twenty-four weeks?'

'Six months! God, yes. Priti is lithe. I'd have noticed if she had a doughnut for lunch.'

'If you were not told, and you could not see a bump, I struggle to believe the CPS will even consider premeditated infanticide. If you hadn't intended to kill the baby, it won't stick. Although, it could add to the harm severity of the attack on Priti. Also, under twenty-four weeks, the foetus isn't viable – you can't kill something that isn't even a baby, yet.'

Jessica leant forward, grabbing a carrier bag and vomiting her coffee and toast.

'You ok?'

Jessica nodded, blowing her nose into the side of the bag.

'Is it, was it, Jason's?

'How should I know? Can't we ask him?'

'This brings me on to my next subject, Jessica. You do not contact Priti or Jason in any way. You do not stalk them on social media, you do not have any of your friends or family approach them, you do not approach his friends or even mutual friends. You do not…'

'Ok! Ok, I get it. I am not sure I have anything to say to them, anyway.'

'I am surprised the police agreed to bail you to an address outside the county. Stay indoors, Jess, remember you are on curfew. Just behave. If your electronic tag bleeps once, you risk arrest. If Priti or Jason raise any concerns about their safety or you contact them, you risk arrest.'

The journey continued in silence. As they pulled off the dual carriageway, Jessica flung the bag of vomit out of the window.

'And don't get arrested for littering.'

Jessica snorted a laugh. They pulled into a road of grand Georgian villas and the car slid gently into the kerb as Mrs Wilson struggled to bring it to a safe stop.

Jessica lay back in the bath. Amara leant against the frame of the open door. Amara's wife pushed past and stood between the two.

'Leave her to have a bath Amara, for Christ's sake!'

Amara raised her eyebrows and signalled for Willow to calm down, using a palm down motion.

'Don't tell me to calm down. I want her dressed around the house and I don't want you in her room, or her in ours!'

Willow pushed back past Amara, slamming a shoulder into her chest.

'She will be ok. We'd planned a quiet Christmas, just the two of us. She became more excited when it snowed. She will be back in the spirit tomorrow. Promise.'

'I will stay in my room tomorrow, Am. I promise I won't get in your way.'

'You will not! I'm doing Akara and Pap for breakfast. Willow is roasting turkey, and I am doing some Abacha as a starter for a late Christmas lunch. We have already wrapped your present...'

'I have got you something, Amara, to share with Willow, but it is in my suitcase at home. Sorry.'

'Don't you fret, girl. I have spoken with your sister. She will check with Jason first, then the two of us will go to yours and pack some clothes and bits. Probably Monday if the roads are ok. Jason will still be in hospital. Swinging the lead if you ask me.'

Jessica smiled at her friend's attempt to lighten the mood. Amara tipped a jug of water over Jessica's head and massaged shampoo into her hair.

'Sorry love, you have nits.'

'No! Fuck. The cell blanket was crawling. Fuck! How embarrassing.'

Willow entered the bathroom again, from her hiding place just out of view. She retrieved a box from the cabinet.

'Don't worry Jessica. I am always bringing home little friends from the class I teach. I will do it Amara.'

Willow pulled over a painted milkmaid's stool and sat next to the bath. She towel-dried Jessica's hair with a damp facecloth, and fine-tooth combed through medicated shampoo. She stopped occasionally to pop a nit between her fingernails. Jessica sobbed. Neither woman interrupted as she cried. Eventually, she wiped her face with wet hands and blew her nose into the bubbles.

'I am so sorry to ruin your Christmas. I could not stay in cells another night. I'd have gone mad. I am claustrophobic, and you know. I am not looking for sympathy, I am just saying. I can't go back to jail. I can't.'

The sobbing began again. Jessica's shoulders heaved as Willow worked on her hair. Tears escaped silently down Amara's cheeks. The doorbell rung, followed immediately by several raps on the knocker.

'I'll go. Amara, dry her hair, but don't rinse the shampoo yet. We'll let it work for a bit.' Willow left the bathroom to return shortly afterwards, as Jessica was slipping on an oversized dressing gown of Amara's. 'It's the police. Parked across our drive with blues flashing. Fucking embarrassing!'

'Miss Khan! You are looking refreshed.'

'This is harassment DC Dolly Williamson! What are you doing here?'

'Do I not get a thank you? For smoothing the way to a family Christmas lunch.'

'Thank you.' Jessica meant for her answer to sound sarcastic, but there was a humble sincerity which the room picked up.

'I don't suppose we could have a private moment to chat?'

'No!' Willow shouted. 'This is my house. Say what you have to say, get your fucking flashing lights off my property, and take your boots off; look at the carpet!'

Jessica made eye contact with Amara, before dropping her chin to her chest. Amara took Willow's elbow, who shook her off and stomped towards the kitchen, followed by Amara and the uniformed officer.

'Lovely house. I bet your friend earns more in a day than I earn in a week.' He smiled. 'Have you seen your bedroom yet? I bet it is warm and tastefully decorated.'

'I have fleas, you dick! What do you want? Say it and fuck off!'

'Or what, Miss Khan? You will fight me and break my bones?'

'Taylor! My name is Taylor. Please leave me alone.'

'We have a deal, Miss Khan. Have you read the Merchant of Venice?'

Jessica realised she was crying again. Tears of frustration.

'Please. Please tell me what you want, and just go.'

'I am an honourable man, Miss Khan. I try to deliver on my side of deals. I will expect you to deliver on yours.' He tapped a text into his phone. The doorbell chimed. 'I'll get it!' he chirped for those who stood in the kitchen.

A second uniformed officer led Jason into the room. He was hunched over and wet with sleet. The walk from the parked squad car had obviously taken some time. Jessica sprang to her feet. She rushed to Jason. He extended an arm to keep her away and as her chest contacted his hand, the force pushed him backwards. The uniform kept him from stumbling and twisted to form a barrier between Jason and Jessica.

'Sit down, Mrs Taylor! Now!'

The uniform shouting brought the three from the kitchen. Amara took Jessica's shoulders and sat her in a dining chair. Willow pulled out a second chair for Jason. She helped him out of his wet coat and lay it on the chair by the log burner to warm. She retrieved a throw from the sofa to wrap around his shoulders.

Jason wore a medical mask. One eye and cheekbone were covered, as was one half of his jaw. He dribbled from the side of his mouth.

'You ok?'

Jason slowly shook his head.

'Priti?'

Jason shrugged. Then shook his head.

'The baby.'

Jason shook his head. 'Dead,' he mumbled, his jaw wired closed.

'I know Jace. Sorry. Was it yours?'

He made eye contact and mumbled, 'It?'

'Sorry. He, she? They?'

'No.' he mumbled.

'No! But you are seeing Priti?'

Jason shook his head.

'But you have been seeing her? You had an affair? You slept with her?'

Jason shook his head again. Jessica stared at her husband, wide eyed.

He slowly mumbled into his teeth, obviously in pain. 'You stupid fucking cow! Her parents had thrown her out. She was scared. She was thinking of having an abortion. She came to you for advice and support. I said she could stay for the night. We were going to Teams you in the morning.'

'I, I thought…'

'I'm flying for *gaforce*. It's *oger*.'

'I don't understand love. Speak slowly.'

Jason reached for a Christmas card and a pen from the table. On the back, he wrote, *I am divorcing you. I never want to see you again.*

Jessica screwed up the card. Jason stood unaided, but swayed, gripping the back of his chair. The second uniform retrieved his coat, and as Jessica went to stand, ordered her to stay sitting. Jason walked, helped, into the squall.

'Miss Khan.'

Jessica shook her head, gulping back bile.

'Leave her alone!' Amara stepped forward.

'Miss Khan, you are on police bail.'

Jessica stared at the DC, slowly nodding.

'There are quite strict conditions attached.'

Jessica struggled to concentrate on the DC. She kept looking towards the front door and the sound of the police car pulling into the freezing slush of the road.

'Miss Khan, sorry, Taylor. I believe you have broken your bail conditions and have met with your husband and alleged victim, Jason Taylor. I witnessed a police officer intervening twice to protect Mr Taylor from you. Mr Taylor himself had to push you away, despite his obvious vulnerability, pain, and discomfort. Mrs Taylor, I am arresting you for serious breaches of your bail conditions.

'No!' Jessica shouted. Amara and Willow moved to Jessica, who now stood clutching a bottle of wine by the neck as a weapon.

'You monster!' yelled Amara. 'You brought Jason here.'

The remaining uniformed police officer rested her hand on her taser. The DC spoke again.

'Amara Pebbles, Willow Pebbles. You can help your friend by having her put down the bottle and surrender to my lawful arrest, including handcuffing by my colleague. Or police will shortly overrun this room, and I will also arrest you both for obstruction. Ok Miss Khan, let's get you in front of the magistrate before we run out of time; see if we can't settle you in, and reserve you some turkey roll for tomorrow.'

Chapter Four

They booked Jessica back into custody, still wearing Amara's dressing gown and a borrowed hi-vis police coat. Willow had given her a pair of rubber gardening shoes as the police marched her, handcuffed, through the front porch and out to the waiting police car. They issued her with a change of clothes at the custody suite. They booked her back out of custody and into the care of two burly court bailiffs. The bailiffs marched her along a tunnel connecting the Police Station with the court's complex.

Jessica sat, shaking with cold and nerves.

'Can you stand Mrs Taylor?'

'Of course, sir.' Jessica stood, one hand gripping the high table. Mrs Wilson glanced up at Jessica and away in embarrassment.

Jessica wore her second police issue of a grey tracksuit. The bailiff, who escorted her to the court, gave her his spare jumper to wear. She still shivered, and her teeth chattered. Her hair hung lank; damp with medicated shampoo.

'Please state your name and date of birth.'

Jessica's voice was mousey and gravelly. The magistrate asked her to speak louder. She cleared her throat and started over.

'Jessica Taylor. 4th May 1985. Sir.'

'And you do not require medical assistance, Mrs Taylor?'

'No sir. I promise I am ok. I am just a bit cold and worried. I have fleas.' Jessica's mousey voice tailed off.

'Sit down, Mrs Taylor. You know where you are? You know who I am?'

Jessica made to stand again to answer, but Mrs Wilson rested a hand on her forearm.

'Yes sir. Of course.'

The magistrate turned to the man sat further along the same bench seat where Jessica and Mrs Wilson sat. The man stood.

'Gerald Smythe, your worships. I am prosecuting this action. My friend Mrs Jacquie Wilson is representing the defendant, Mrs Jessica Taylor.'

Mrs Wilson stood and bowed to the front of court and sat again.

Smythe continued. 'You will see my written submission, your worships. We have no witnesses to call. May I remind your worships, your copy of the submission has a name of a serving police officer, which is redacted from the submission published to the open court.'

The head magistrate glanced at the court's Legal Advisor, who nodded back her agreement.

Smythe continued. 'You will see from our submission that Mrs Taylor has been brought back into custody for failing to comply with police bail requirements. We ask this court to remand Mrs Taylor for a maximum of 28 days. During that period, the police will look to complete outstanding enquiries, prepare any file for Crown Prosecution, and charge Mrs Taylor as appropriate.'

The magistrate looked at Mrs Wilson as Smythe took his seat. Mrs Wilson stood to address the court. The magistrate saw Jessica drop her chin and shake more violently. He spoke, so Mrs Wilson took her seat again.

'Usher, please find Mrs Taylor a blanket and some water. This is a cold and uninviting environment for you, Mrs Taylor. Bear with us.' Jessica nodded. 'Mrs Wilson, I hope you have a better grasp of this than I do!' He waved Smythe's submission.

Mrs Wilson rose again. 'Thank you, your honour. Indeed. It reads like a Kafkaesque travesty. My client was released on police bail to appear again at Portsmouth Central Police Station as required. She duly reported to her agreed bail address, where she conducted herself properly and in total compliance with her bail conditions. Your worships will have read how three police officers attended the address, uninvited and without prior notice. The officers also accompanied Mrs Taylor's husband to that same address to meet with Mrs Taylor, despite this contradicting the bail requirements. I understand from my client…'

'Mrs Wilson, we will give you a chance to further expand on your client's understanding, presently. For the moment, please only address this written submission.'

Mrs Wilson rose again. 'Of course, your honour. Once Mr Taylor had visited, one officer took him away again. Mrs Taylor was arrested by DC X for breaking her bail conditions, by meeting with her husband, whom DC X had unilaterally brought to the address. Kafkaesque indeed, your honour. And may I suggest cruel and unjust?'

'No Mrs Wilson, you may not. Mr Smythe?'

'I have nothing further to add, your honour. We request Mrs Taylor is remanded in custody following the breaking of bail conditions. We are not looking to scrutinise the police investigation or the actions of individual officers. Your worships will have noted that the original alleged crime, bailed, is indictable.'

'Mrs Wilson?'

'My client played no role in the breaking of bail conditions, other than that of a victim. She runs her own business, and her own household. We request the prosecution's submission is rejected and my client released to the original bail conditions or released without bail, as your worships see fit. My client has already lodged a complaint with the Superintendent regarding DC X's behaviour.'

'Mrs Taylor, you may remain seated, if you wish.' Jessica shook her head and stood, now swamped by the borrowed jumper and court blanket. 'Do you have your own children to care for? Or any other children or adults?' Jessica shook her head. 'Can you speak out to the court, Mrs Taylor?'

'Sorry. No, I am not caring for any children or adults, sir.'

'Your business, Mrs Taylor. What do you do and are you busy over this Christmas period?'

'I am an engineering consultant, sir. I contract to Company based here in Portsmouth. In the Naval Base. I have been working away in India and that contract has finished. I am suspended from applying for a new contract whilst under investigation for this assault, sir. The victim of the assault, Priti Khan, is a staff employee of Company, and my husband is also a contractor.'

The magistrate let out a long sigh, glancing at Mrs Wilson. Mrs Wilson went to stand, but the magistrate held up a hand and shook his head.

'We have heard enough. Thank you, Mrs Wilson.'

The court's Legal Advisor approached the three magistrates with an open reference book. The four discussed paragraphs in hushed voices.

'Please.' The head magistrate addressed the court again. Smythe, Mrs Wilson, and Jessica stood. 'You are not here today to face criminal charges, Mrs Taylor. Contravening bail requirements is not a criminal offence, there is no charge to answer. Further, we hold deep concerns regarding the conduct of this police investigation and the influence and involvement of one DC X and Special Branch, generally.' Mrs Wilson and Jessica glanced at each other, at the mention of Special Branch. 'We have left a note on file to ask your appearance before this court, upon your being charged with any crime, is expedited. We will write to the Crown and raise concerns about the management of your bail, asking for your Plea and Trial Preparation Hearing to be arranged promptly, once referred, and that your bail status is further reviewed as a priority, at that time. Today, we will write to the Chief Superintendent concerning the conduct of DC X and will request the constabulary to investigate and report back to this court, initially within one week. Do you understand, Mrs Taylor? Please speak up.'

'Yes, sir.'

'However, you are here for us to consider the breaking of bail conditions. You are required not to meet with your husband, or indeed Priti Khan, for any reason outside of the court's jurisdiction. You met with your husband, contrary to your bail conditions, despite the spurious and, frankly, quite scurrilous circumstances. Unfortunately, Mrs Taylor, we have no choice but to find for the prosecution. You are remanded in custody to appear in front of this court weekly, for a maximum of twenty-eight days.'

Jessica caught hold of Mrs Wilson's arm and slipped back into her chair, sobbing.

'I could have cried, Gerald. The poor woman is in shock. Her world is imploding.'

'She probably should have thought of that before trying to kill three people, Jax.'

46

'It is me you are talking to now, Gerald.'

Smythe shrugged. 'Shall we grab a room, Jax? For old time's sake?'

'How's Brenda? Tomorrow's lunch prepared?'

Smythe laughed. 'Suit yourself.'

'I'll say *what*, for old time's sake, Gerald. *What* is going on here? Attempted murder? Unlikely. Infanticide? No chance. Special Branch? What the fuck!'

'They only brought us in for the bail hearing, Jax. Coffee?'

Mrs Wilson watched Smythe drop coins into the machine and select a white coffee with sugar.

'I don't take sugar, numpty. You knew me well enough to sleep with me, but you don't know how I take it?'

'I remember exactly how you take it, Jax.'

'Cherish that thought. We won't be doing it again. Ever.'

'Ok. So would you like the benefit of my experience?'

'I just said no, Gerald. And being old differs from experience.'

Smythe laughed. 'Ouch! Are the two things even related, Jax? We have a bored DI thinking he can slip in an attempted murder to boost his 2022 clear-up rates. And separate from that, we have DC Dolly playing games. Do you know your sweet young woman very well? What has she got to lose and what has she got to offer Dolly?'

'She has everything to lose, Gerald. I mean everything. She has lost most of it already, and she only has one more thing worth taking away.'

'Suicide watch?'

'I meant her liberty. But, although I haven't run up the flag yet, yes, I think maybe a suicide risk. She had a lot to live for and now she hasn't. I'm not sure she will be any good at keeping canaries in Portsmouth's Kingston nick for twenty years.'

'Do canaries live to twenty? But what has she got to offer DC X?'

'No idea. But the DC is on borrowed time.'

'Not for my money. Whatever he is doing is probably more important than a sadistic little bitch losing a bit of bail.'

'She is wild, Gerald, but she really isn't sadistic.'

'I bet Mr T and his bit of fluff will disagree.'

'Apparently, they weren't shagging. Jessica was overreacting.'

'*Overreacting!* There's an understatement. I will see you in court on that one, Jax.'

'Are you taking it on?'

'Probably. If it is *attempted*. We aren't interested in common assault.'

'I can't wait for disclosure.'

Smythe kissed the top of her head.

'I'm not saying I would let you in on anything I know, Jax. But what I will say is, I know nothing at the moment.'

'Don't be a stranger, Gerald. Mrs T is going down for something, just don't let it be for the wrong crime. If I hear anything about DC X, I will let you know. And you will reciprocate?'

Smythe waved over his head as he left the vending room.

Chapter Five

'Jess. I am going to have you transferred to remand at Kingston Prison under your maiden name.'

'Don't you start. DC Dolly Williams insists on calling me Miss Khan.'

'I think it is for the best. Do not trust anyone inside, not even the officers. If they hear about you kicking a pregnant girl and the baby aborting, well, you know. Things could get worse for you. The prison governor will know your married name is Taylor, but she will be keen to comply with using your maiden name for a simple life. Hopefully, no one will make the connection.

'Listen Jess, chin up. Ok? This is absolutely not what we wanted, but it is what it is. I will talk to Amara Pebbles and arrange for some clothes. I will transfer a little money into your prison account. Keep smiling, eh? I'm sorry about this, really sorry. I will work on an appeal Tuesday and will keep you posted.'

Jessica remained in the court cells for a further twelve hours, waiting for prison transport. The empty cells had been deep cleaned for the holidays, and she was the only guest. Her cell had an open toilet and a tiny metal hand basin with cold water only. She asked for shampoo and towels, but on receiving none, she sponged some of the medicated shampoo from her hair, drying it on her blanket. Without a hairbrush, she spent much of the night trying to force her fingers through matted hair.

Wearing the bailiff's jumper and wrapped in the now damp court blanket, Jessica climbed into the back of the freezing, unheated *sweatbox* prison van. The journey to Portsmouth's Kingston Prison promised to be brief. She lay her head against the heavily tinted bulletproof glass, glimpsing lights, and the occasional road sign between the thick bars. The retrofitted Mercedes Sprinter sped through Fratton and Milton to the Prison.

The van crawled through airlock double gates before parking in a floodlit garage. The driver of the van completed paperwork at a kiosk window before the rear van doors eventually opened. The guard then opened a second cage door and unlocked Jessica's manacles, leaving her to climb out of the van wearing handcuffs. He removed the handcuffs once inside the secure reception area.

'Welcome to HMP Kingston, Portsmouth, Miss Khan. And a Merry Christmas to you.'

'Thank you. Merry Christmas.'

The room was heated and bright; the staff working in short-sleeved white shirts, but Jessica still felt a chill to her bones. Her blood having thinned in India, she imagined waking early on Christmas morning to sneak downstairs before Jason woke. She would light the log burner, retrieve smoked salmon and prosecco from the fridge, and skip back upstairs for Christmas bubbles and sex in their warm bed. Instead, Jessica now answered a series of questions concerning her health and wellbeing.

'Ok Miss Khan. You are a prison virgin?'

Jessica felt vulnerable and scared, choosing not to answer the sexualised question.

'We are quiet this morning, Jess, it being Christmas and all. And I am in a good mood, so don't ruin it. If I ask you a question, you answer it first time. There's a love.'

'Sorry. Yes. I have not been in a prison before.'

'Pop in there. Pop your clothes off. Time to meet the boss.'

'I don't have a bra or anything. No pants, like. I was arrested in just a dressing gown.'

The prison officer laughed. 'You women crack me up, you really do. Everything off, down to your birthday suit. Quick as you can.'

Jessica stripped, standing in the bright lights of a separate room without a door. The officer pointed to a large metal chair shaped like a medieval torture machine.

'Miss Khan, meet the B.O.S.S Chair. Take a seat. This Body Orifice Security Scanner reduces the amount of fumbling I need to do in your orifices. Now, last chance, do you have anything secreted?'

'No. Nothing.'

'Good girl. Now let's do a bit of hands-on-old-school.'

'Please. I…'

'Don't forget – no making me repeat myself.'

Jessica stood under the bright medical lamp as the officer snapped on a clean pair of rubber gloves.

'Right. So, let's see if I can't remember the correct order to do this. Mouth open.'

Jessica opened her mouth as the officer placed two fingers inside, brushed around her cheeks and manipulated her tongue. Jessica's teeth chattered again, and she was worried she might involuntarily bite down on the officer's fingers. She cried as quietly as possible.

'Good girl. I always remember Office of Public Affairs. Oral, Pussy, Anal.' The officer laughed at her own joke. 'You wouldn't want me to get that wrong now, would you? Kneel on the stool, arms and torso on the bed. Well done. Nearly over. Goodness, what's going on here?'

'I haven't been since the flight from India.'

'We can't be having that now, can we? The lube will help. Can you take laxatives?'

Jessica nodded.

'You are doing it again.'

'Sorry, miss. Yes miss, please. It's just there was no door on the loo in the nick. I can't go if I think someone might see. I'll be ok once I get to my own room.'

The officer snorted into a genuine belly laugh.

'*Own room!* Crack me up, honestly, you crack me up. Now shower and dress in these.'

'But I'm on remand. Can't I wear my own clothes? Miss.'

'Darling, you haven't brought any, now have you, love? These will see you through until next week.'

Jessica showered in the adjacent bathroom, again with no door fitted. There was hardly any water pressure, the water lukewarm. She had to lean against the shower control button with one hand and wash with the other. The soap smelt carbolic, and she tried again to wash more of the medicated shampoo from her matted hair. She towel-dried. The officer gave her a hairbrush – not much bigger or more substantial than a child's dolly brush. The officer nodded to the toilet in one corner; brightly lit and with no seat fitted onto the porcelain. Jessica declined.

They escorted her onto the wing and to the central office. A senior prison officer asked a few cursory questions about Jessica's health and risks before pointing to a seat at an empty desk. The sound of keys releasing a heavy lock echoed along the otherwise silent landing. A woman in her mid-forties was escorted to the seat opposite Jessica, wearing a jumper and jeans, which Jessica could see pulled over cotton pyjamas.

'What sort of time do you call this, bitch?'

'Sorry, miss. I was being held at the court…'

'Hey, don't cry, love. I was only pulling your leg. And don't call me miss, I'm just a slag like you. My name is Ingrid. I am your *Insider*. What is your name?

'Jessica Khan, 4th May 1985.'

The woman laughed, gently placing her hand against Jessica's cheek. This gentle act caught in Jessica's throat and her tears streamed.

'Just Jessica will do, love.'

'Jess. If you like, please Ingrid.'

'Let's run through a few things, Jess. I'm here to let you know how things work. There are only seventy-seven of us on this wing; I am sure we will see each other during association. You can sit with me during Christmas lunch, if you want. Nothing I say can be repeated to the cons or the screws, ok? I don't want to get a name for snitching or gossiping. Understood? But you can ask me anything – which doesn't mean I can, or will, answer. First piece of advice – don't tell anyone why you are here. It is none of their business and they will not feel offended if you politely decline to answer. And don't start making up things to make yourself sound bigger, either. Nothing you might have to live up to. Are you serving sentence or remand? We are a mixed wing. What got you in here?'

'Remand for twenty-eight days, hopefully less. I thought my husband was fucking his bestie, so I slapped them both. Harder than I meant to.'

Ingrid doubled with laughter, bringing her head to bang lightly on the table.

'So how is the *don't tell anyone why you are here* rule going?'

'Shit!' Jessica brought her hands to her face.

'You are a pretty one, Jess. No, I mean a really pretty one.'

'Thank you.'

'I meant it as a warning love, not a compliment. Tread carefully,'

The heavy door slammed behind her. Jessica stood in the centre of the cell, facing the high window. Below the window sat a shelf holding a large plastic bottle. Under the shelf stood a bucket. To her left was a single steel bed, a figure under the blankets. To her right stood bunk beds. The upper bunk held a mattress folded in two. The bottom bunk had a board bolted across the full length to form a rough table. A few personal items stood neatly arranged on the board, with a small flat screen television.

'Who are you?'

'Jessica.'

'Why?'

'Why am I Jessica?'

'You taking the piss? Why are you here?'

'No, sorry. I thought you meant… This is the cell they brought me to.'

'Oh, clever cow. Why are you inside, idiot?'

'It's a long story. Is this my bunk?'

'No. My boyfriend stays in that one, when I have finished shagging him. You can watch if you like.'

Jessica straightened the mattress and made her bed.

'Don't stand on my table!'

'Sorry. Look, I need to use the loo.'

'You just got here. Wait for association. I am not eating my Christmas breakfast with the bucket stinking of your piss.'

Jessica's stomach cramped. 'Shit! It's not piss. I can't wait.' She moved towards the alarm button.

'No! you can't push that, just to go for a shit. There isn't room service. The screws will be pissed.'

Jessica pulled down her joggers and squatted over the bucket. 'God, I'm so sorry.'

'No! Wait, you dirty bitch!' The cellmate jumped from her bed and retrieved a man's rugby sock from a wooden locker. 'Use this. Double bubble.'

'What? You're fucking kidding!'

'Use the sock, or I'll ram that turd so far back up your arse you'll be able to polish it when you brush your teeth!'

'Jesus Christ.'

Jessica snatched the sock and stretched it wide as the first solid lump of faeces forced its way out. She clenched her eyes closed with pain at the same time as clenching everything else. The laxatives proved effective as she continued to fill the sock, her eyes watering and sweat pouring down her neck. The cell mate cackled, kicking her feet with amusement. Jessica's breathing regulated as the last emptied into the sock, her cramping stomach rumbling and gurgling. She wiped herself on the inside of the sock.

'Sorry, where is the toilet roll?'

The cellmate continued to laugh hysterically, returning from the locker with a half roll of toilet paper.

'Double fucking bubble! And three-ply soft quilted, none of this John Wayne!' She held it out of Jessica's reach, waiting for a response.

'Yes, whatever you said, just give me the loo roll.'

Jessica finished and stretched upright, tying the sock in a knot.

'Not in the bucket, you dirty cow. Chuck your shit parcel out of the window!'

Shaking with discomfort, embarrassment, and frustration, Jessica climbed onto her bunk. Opening the cracked, metal framed, upper hopper window, she threw out the full sock. It only fell as far as a coil of rusting barbed wire, hanging in view of the main cell window. Closing the icing window against the penetrating wind took Jessica several attempts; barely able to reach it with her outstretched arm.

'How's your first day in paradise?'

'Fucking great, Ingrid. Thanks. I'm sharing my cell with a neandertal, and half the wing heard me give birth this morning.'

Ingrid threw back her head, laughing.

'Ingrid, what is double bubble and what the fuck is John Wayne?'

'Double bubble is paying back twice what you borrowed – like the interest. John Wayne is the hard skidding prison toilet paper – hard, like John Wayne. What do you owe Naomi?'

'Naomi? I can't think of a prettier name for a less pretty individual.'

'Naomi is just a cell warrior, Jess. Stand up to her. But don't push it; she sucks up to some dangerous people.'

'Where is the shop to buy Naomi's replacement stores? I guess I owe a pair of men's rugby socks and two loo rolls.'

'The canteen shop isn't open until Friday. Up to you, but I might give you two socks or something instead – maybe some biscuits. And I can let you have some loo roll to pay her back. But then you'll owe me double bubble – four socks and four loo rolls. Most of us keep men's socks for emergencies. It's a thing. That's how it works, sorry. Anything else? Toothpaste? More pants?'

The couple walked along the lower landing to Ingrid's cell for the supplies. They then went on to the gathering crowd, sitting ready for the first of two Christmas films.

'The Great Escape! You are joking!' Jessica managed a laugh for the first time in days.

'How was the kedgeree?'

'Kedgeree? A cold fishfinger squashed into hard rice, with a boiled egg and watery curry sauce?'

Ingrid studied Jessica for some time. 'I like you, Jess. You are clever, witty, and still have a tan. But today's breakfast was a welcomed treat from months of blandness and repetitiveness. I don't want you coming across to the girls as entitled or snooty. Being disliked spreads like hysteria. Don't be everyone's best friend, but show some respect.'

'Sure. Of course. Sorry.'

'Hey, see those two?'

'Oh my God! Twins?'

Jessica followed Ingrid's nod to two early middle-aged women walking towards the group, holding hands. They wore identical beige dungarees and brown Velcro training shoes. They also wore identical thick cardigans, had short gingery hair and bottle bottom wire spectacles. Ingrid laughed into Jessica's shoulder.

'No, they are married. They met in nick.'

'No way! Is that even allowed?'

'Absolutely, we have our rights. But I agree, they have married themselves. This is a funny story, talking about hysteria inside. At the start of the covid pandemic, these two numbskulls staggered onto the landing for association, feeling ill. They had slept ok, but at the exact moment the cells were opened, they both felt nauseous. They stumbled out of cells disorientated, blurred vision, and could not walk straight. One complained of migraine.' Ingrid laughed at the recollection.

'Doesn't sound funny.'

'Honestly Jess, you had to be there. The prisoners were running around like headless chickens. In those days we thought covid would sweep through and kill us all.'

Ingrid continued laughing, finding it more difficult to repeat her account of the event. Jessica shook her head, not sure if to laugh or feel horrified by those trapped in the situation.

'Association was cancelled. They locked us down into isolation, whilst whisking away this married couple to the medical wing. By lunchtime, thirty-five other inmates had gone down with similar symptoms and the governor declared an emergency. The navy sent in a fully staffed field hospital.'

'Did everyone survive?'

This comment sent Ingrid into choking giggles, so loud the other inmates turned to watch the couple.

'It was all hysteria, Jess. Everyone was perfectly healthy.'

'Except the original married couple?'

'They had accidentally swapped spectacles when getting out of bed, and each was wearing the wrong prescription. In the medical wing, the medic told them to remove their glasses for examination, and they both made an immediate and full recovery,'

'No!' Jessica joined in the laughing.

The film show was rowdy. The inmates cheered the prisoners in the film, whilst booing the guards. Conversely, the prison officers cheered the Germans and booed the prisoners. Before lunch, Jessica took a deep breath and forced herself to use the landing toilet.

The bathroom was through an open arch without doors, near the fortified central office. The individual toilets sat in a row two meters apart, with no cubicles or any dividing walls. Jessica passed one occupied toilet, avoiding eye contact, concentrating on the last toilet in the row. Even sitting on the furthest toilet from the *door*, she could clearly see, and be seen, from the landing.

'Merry Christmas, love. What's your name?'

'Merry Christmas. My name is Jessica. Your name?' Jessica avoided eye contact with her fellow bathroom mate.

'Horrible first time, love. It gets easier, promise.'

Jessica nodded, before blushing deeply and staring at her feet as the last of the laxatives worked through.

As DC Dolly Williamson promised, lunch was turkey roll, consisting more of cheap salty pig than reconstituted turkey. The excitement in the mess area was palpable. All eyes turned to the opened barred door leading to the kitchen. Headed by a beaming young woman in stained chef's whites, a line of prisoners and officers appeared carrying metal trays, to cheers from the inmates. The young chef took a bow and took her place at Jessica's table.

The gravy was watery, the roast potatoes reheated from fresh or from frozen, and the peas tinned. But the carrots were crisp and carefully arranged into wigwam shapes on each plate. Cauliflower was white and slightly al dente, and the cabbage lightly fried with garlic and tiny flecks of freshly roasted chestnuts.

Jessica spoke to the young chef across the table. 'Did you do this? It is lovely, thank you. The Yorkshire pudding is perfect and cauli is my favourite.'

'Thank you. I hope you enjoy it and Merry Christmas.' Everyone within earshot chimed in with a Merry Christmas, aimed more at the young cook and each other than at Jessica. 'The prison provided the turkey for today as the meat, but nothing extra. Everyone here has had to scrimp on daily food to collect enough for this.'

Jessica smiled and thanked her again. When the others were all chatting, Ingrid whispered to Jessica.

'It might not seem much, but the peas, yorkies, slices of sausage, and the garlic were all scavenged from other day's meals. This young lady has just one pound and ninety-eight pence worth of food to feed each of us each day, but she wrings out any morsel of flavour. The inmate gardeners all work extra hard to supplement the veggies, since this young lady took over the cooking. They only have tiny squares of dead soil in which to scratch around. Tomorrow, it is back to standing in line for slops. In twenty-seven days, Jess, I will ask if you miss the squashed-fishfinger-in-rice breakfast-in-bed.'

At the mention of twenty-seven days remaining, Jessica gave an involuntary shudder.

The entire wing watched Wizard of Oz in the afternoon, singing along to the songs. The senior officer shouted for lockup and the inmates formed a rowdy conga, singing The Yellow Brick Road and dropping each prisoner back to their own cell. Officers tensed and shot glances between the mob of prisoners and the senior prison officer, but the high jinks ended peacefully. The last of the inmates jigged their way home.

Chapter Six

Mrs Wilson visited Jessica on the following Tuesday, bringing two 70cmx55cmx25cm boxes of clothing, food, toiletries, and other supplies. Jessica asked for scented sanitary bags as a gift for Naomi, but the prison ban bags from the wing as an asphyxiator. The senior prison officer signed off the amended prisoner property card, and the parcel waited for Jessica in her cell. Mrs Wilson also maxed out Jessica's charge card at £10 and paid for a prison phone card with the maximum credit of £10.

'Anything I can do for you, Jess?'

'Get me out of here.'

'We are working on it.'

'You are my first visitor, Jacquie. I am such a pariah.'

'I know Amara and your brother-in-law have applied to visit. A cousin submitted a third application, but I am not sure of the name. The prison is checking backgrounds, but nothing will happen quickly over the holidays. Hopefully, I will have you out soon. Do you feel safe?'

'There are a lot of criminals in here, Jax.' Both women managed a thin smile. 'I am ok. Some girls are really sweet. My cellmate thinks she is a bit of a gangster, but she hasn't threatened me or anything. If she did, I would just punch her lights out.'

'That will look good at your bail hearing.'

'The food is shit. There is a *twelve-year-old* doing her best, but the prison has all the taste removed before cooking. Brian, my dog, wouldn't eat it. Male or female cousin? We aren't that close.'

'Twelve? They say you know you are getting old when the prisoners look young. Talking of policemen, I am assuming you have had no more visits? Not from our helpful DC Dolly Williamson?'

'Nothing. Should I have?'

'No. Just get a message to me if he approaches you again.'

'How are the lovebirds?'

'They are the actual victims here, Jess. Don't be so glib. Both are due out of the hospital today. Your sister has Brian for a couple of days until Jason can cope.'

'Poor dog. I know how it must feel. I bet he has to shit in a sock in case it marks the lawn.'

'Sorry, Jess?'

'I know you are working hard and doing everything you can, Jax.'

'But?'

'But you need to do more. I am not sleeping. I can't eat. I am going downhill fast. I am having night-terrors and anxiety attacks. The screws told Naomi and me to stand by our bunks whilst they did a routine search. I thought she was going to strip search me again and I couldn't breathe, like hyperventilating or something.'

'I can have the prison surgeon…'

'Don't patronise me, Jax. I don't need a doctor. I need to be out of here. I am innocent.'

'Innocent of what, Jess?'

'Innocent until proven guilty! Perhaps the DI was correct – I need a brief who knows the law!'

'We are doing our best. I promise. Look, I will chase for the prison visits. They took the family photos out of your parcel because some had pictures of the *victim,* Jason, and your nieces. I will get them sorted and re-bundled.'

'Yeah, right. Just photos of me on my own or with Brian. Is the dog classed as a victim? I tell you what – just concentrate on getting me out.'

'I promise…'

'No Jax, I will promise you something. You get me out of here or I will get myself out. In a box if necessary.' Jessica rose and walked towards the visiting room door. She mumbled, 'Thanks for the stuff.'

'Two visitors in one day! And you only had to pay one of them to come.'

'Who is this one, Miss?'

'Your cousin.'

'Which one, boss?'

'Parton.'

'Parton, Miss? Man or woman?'

The prison officer stopped to stare at Jessica.

'You don't have a cousin called Parton? Do you know anyone called Parton, Khan?'

'Sorry Miss, only messing. Yes, I have several cousins, male and female, with the name Parton.'

'First name or last?'

'Um. Kind of both. It is a last name, but it's a tradition to keep it as a first or middle name, especially if it is a girl who changes her surname on getting married. And then they might …' Jessica blushed but maintained eye contact.

The officer stared at Jessica for a moment longer before continuing the journey.

'Well, you know him well enough to get twenty minutes in the conjugal suite.'

'*Dolly Parton*. You really are a scream, Detective Constable of the Special Branch.'

'You signed to verify and agree to see me, Miss Khan. A compulsive rule breaker, aren't you just?'

'I am calling my brief later. She is keen to know when you turn up.'

'You can't quite bring yourself to put all your eggs into her basket, can you? Still hedging your bets?'

'What *do* you want, DC Williamson?'

'I thought you offered to help me, Miss Khan. All I want you to do is fulfil your side of the bargain.'

'You got me out for a couple of hours. I didn't even have time to rinse my hair, you shitbag. I owe you nothing.'

'The Dolly giveth and the Dolly taketh away.'

'You fuck with my head to prove how powerful you are?'

'You kick a pregnant woman half to death for photographing your husband in a swimming pool.'

'I'm out of here. Fuck you.'

'Sit down. I am running out of the time I can waste on you. If you want to spend another twenty-four days in here on bail, then another ten months on remand, then another six, ten, or twenty years on sentence, then sure, let us agree to part ways.'

'What are you offering me, DC Shitbag?'

'It's not all about you. Don't you want to know what you can do for me first?'

'Same thing. Now get on with it.'

The DC sat back in his chair. Jessica imagined she could hear the cogs in his head churn and clatter.

'Information is power, Miss Khan. I want information.'

'What can I tell you?'

'Oh, are we back talking about Jessica already? I want information about a terrible, catastrophic incident. Before it happens.'

'What do I know about anything?'

'The more I know you, Miss Khan, the more I realise you know so little about anything, much.'

'Flattery will get you everywhere.'

'I want you to keep close to someone who I am monitoring.'

'And then grass them to the filth? I still have my pride, *cunt-stable*.'

'Look at you, with your newfound honour amongst thieves!'

'If, and this is only an *if*, what do I receive in return? What guarantees do I get? I want my brief to sit in on any agreement.'

'Bless. No brief, nothing in writing. When this is over, you move back to your beach shack in Turkey under your own name. You live for a couple of years off a pension, equivalent to that of a retired Turkish teacher. Not much, admittedly, but it will give you room to start again. You are still young. Or you can go into our witness protection scheme in the UK, somewhere. Let's talk about the detail when this is over.'

'Let's talk about the detail now. Shall we?'

'The thing is, Miss Khan, I am banking on the third option. Save a few bob on my budget.'

'Which is?'

'That you probably won't survive.'

'Wow! You really know how to sell a scheme, don't you?'

'I don't need to sell it to you, Miss Khan. I need to sell it to my boss and his masters, but you are already sold, aren't you?'

'You reckon?'

'Take a punt and risk dying in the fresh air. Or stay locked up, and risk dying in here. Or worse, risk staying alive in here. One day in the future, or perhaps even posthumously, you might receive a letter from the King to add to that medal the Turks gave you.'

'I am still not agreeing with this, and I am still talking to my brief about you. But if I agree to do a little snooping around, you will need to prime me first. And this lot in here mustn't suspect, or they'll beat me up, or worse.'

'The next time we meet, Miss Khan, it will all be over. Everything you need to know - I am about to tell you. So, listen carefully.'

'I am not necessarily …'

'I said listen carefully. You can ponder it as much as you like later in your cell. Or tomorrow in your cell. Or next year. Or next decade.'

'Ok. But I want guarantees, or any deal is off.'

Dolly ignored her.

'You don't want to go onto the prisoner protection wing with the nonces.'

'Obviously! Why would I?'

'You would be better on the top security restricted wing.'

'What are you talking about?'

'I am a big believer in identifying the decision makers in life. I am sure you agree. When you do, stick close. Go along for the ride. The entire ride, Miss Khan. Don't get off the train until I call you off. Understood?'

'No, fuck this. I am not convinced. I want Jacquie Wilson here.'

'Did you hear me though, Miss Khan? Did you just hear what I said?'

'Yes. But…'

'Have you seen one of these before, Miss Khan?'
Dolly opened a metal spectacle case taken from his
inside jacket pocket. He handed Jessica the contents.

'What is it? A turkey baster? How the fuck did you
get that past security?'

'Here, let me show you.'

Dolly took back the oversized surgical-steel syringe.
He lent over the table and pulled Jessica's top up over
her chest and scrunched it under her chin. Before she
could protest, he held the tool to below her clavicle
and fired the syringe into the upper swell of her
exposed right breast. Jessica screamed with pain,
jumping to her feet, and backing away in one fluid
movement. Dolly followed her as she stumbled,
pushing her to the floor. He picked up Jessica's fallen
chair and threw it at Jessica's chest. Jessica screamed
again in pain and fear as Dolly also shouted for the
guard, who had already opened the door on hearing
Jessica scream.

'Quick, officer!' shouted Dolly, 'Mrs Taylor fell
over. Is she ok? Are you ok Jessica? What happened?
Are you ok? Help up Mrs Taylor, quickly?'

'What happened, Miss Khan?'

'Nothing *happened*, boss. I stood to say goodbye to
my cousin. I tripped and fell.'

'Your cousin … Mr Parton?'

'Yes, boss.'

'Your cousin … Adolphus Parton, must have friends in high places. His background checks were fast tracked over the holidays.'

Jessica shrugged. 'We aren't that close really, boss. I have lost track of what he does. Sweet of him to make the effort to see me.'

'The prison surgeon says you have a puncture wound to your chest. Did that happen on the wing, or when you fell?'

'When I fell, boss. I rolled onto the foot of my chair. I should sue you. Sorry boss, just joking.'

'No problems on the wing, Jessica?'

'None, boss. I love it. The food is great, but I have a poor view from my room.'

'You aren't missing much. The back of a Victorian hospital, or a bleak wintery city graveyard. If you have any problems, Jessica, you must report it. Some things are best nipped in the bud.'

'I will be fine, boss. I should be out of here soon.'

'That's what they all say.'

'I'll be out before you, boss.'

The two women kept eye contact for a few more seconds.

'Ok, take her back to the wing.'

The prisoners were already locked down for the evening by the time guards escorted Jessica back to her cell. Lights were still on, but Naomi slept on her bed, snoring. Jessica brushed her teeth and washed in the cold water from the toilet bottle. She showered each day but tried to remain naked for as little time as possible in the communal bathhouse. She had taken to rushing her lunch, giving any jelly or biscuits to Ingrid, before rushing off to use the bathroom whilst the others were still eating.

'I'm already missing the fishfinger kedgeree breakfast. These sausages are totally inedible. They are fatty water and some sort of chemical.'

Ingrid nodded in agreement. 'You know how they collect all the slops and muck from an abattoir floor to make dog food? Well, they make prison sausages out of the muck that isn't good enough to make the dog food. Who is the guy you met with yesterday?'

'I met my brief.'

'After her.'

'Blimey. Good job I am not trying to have an affair. Few secrets in here.'

'None. Who is he? A pig?'

'My cousin.'

'Apparently, he smells like a pig, looks like a pig, and oinks like a pig. So, he probably is a pig.'

'I don't think he is. He's a distant cousin. I am not sure. I didn't ask.'

'But you are still under investigation?'

'Yeah. And I am sure the police will interview me again. I have nothing to hide from you. I would say if he was a *fed*, honest.

'Look, changing the subject. Those three keep looking at me.'

74

'Shit, Jessica. They are bad news. They think they run this wing, and to be honest, they pretty much do. Keep out of their way. They will know all about your mystery visitor.'

'He is not a mystery! He is my cousin.'

'They are a stir-family. The one who looks like Mike Tyson's ugly sister is Michelle Adams. Also known as Shelly. She's the daddy. The wife is Natasha Romanoff, aka the Black Widow. Barbie is the daughter. All bloody psychos. Keep clear of them.'

'A family? What, like in a relationship?'

'It's an institutionalised thing, especially with lifers and long sentences. I guess they crave normality, weirdos.'

'But they have sex?'

Shelly and Nats probably do. I understand they are straight, outside, but in here they play a role. Not Barbie, of course.'

'Sorry, why *of course*?'

'Because she is the daughter. I just explained that. She strops around, refusing to do her homework or eat her greens, and the other two *parent* her.'

'No way.'

'They tell her to wash behind her ears and give her pocket money or whatever. She draws them pictures and does chores around the cell.'

'Christ! Diagnosed?'

'They are perfectly healthy for sociopaths. If any of them get out, they will probably revert to normality.'

'And they are dangerous?'

'Not because of that specifically, although they are a fighting unit. They see themselves as vigilantes. They have their own version of law and justice. If anyone breaks their moral code, they deal the punishment. Then they extort a payment from their victim or from the person they feel was wronged.

'Let's say they hear I have pinched your tampons or something. They give me a hiding, return your fanny bullets, then charge *you* a fee for *them* doing the dirty on *me*. Or, say, they think you are grassing to the filth, like your cousin or something. They give you a clip around the ear and fine *you* for breaking *their* rules.'

'He is just my cousin.'

'Keep out of their way. I have warned you. You are fresh, pretty, and suspicious. Exactly their target for some sexual roleplay or extortion.'

Jessica visited the gym for the first time, pumping weights until her limbs and lungs ached. She washed back in her cell and lay on her bunk before lunch.

'Shelly and Nats want a word.'

'I don't know Shelly or Nats, Naomi. But thanks for the offer.'

'Well, they know you.'

'It's a small wing. But thanks for the message.'

'Don't mess with me, bitch.'

'What's up, Naomi? Scared of the Adams family?'

'I am not scared of no one. They are my friends.'

'They know where I am, if they want a word.'

Naomi stood on the cabin bunk table and loomed over Jessica. Her breath stank of sausage fat.

'You are dead pretty, Jess. I don't want them breaking those sexy looks of yours.'

'Get out of my space, weirdo! I like men. I don't mind women, but I don't do ugly!'

Jessica pushed Naomi away.

Ingrid and her two friends sat squashed into two spare places at the adjacent mess table. The Adams family's usual seats remained empty, but they now sat where Ingrid and her friends normally sat with Jessica. Ingrid caught Jessica's eye for a moment before dropping her gaze to her plate, blushing deeply and noticeably squirming in her seat. Jessica collected her meal and, with few options, sat with the Adams in her normal place.

'Don't you want that? I love burgers.'

'Um yes. I do want it, actually. You can have the jelly, if you like.'

Barbie leant over, ignoring Jessica, speared her burger with a fork, and stole the food. Others around tried not to look. Jessica felt both intimidated and embarrassed by her own inaction.

'Can I help you guys? Naomi said you want a word.'

Natasha spoke. 'Just thought we would say hello and welcome you to our wing.'

'Thank you. I appreciate that.'

Shelly spoke. 'That pig you met isn't from Pompey. Who is he?'

'I haven't spoken to the police since coming inside.'

'Don't fuck with me.'

'Honestly. Off the wing I have seen my brief, my cousin, the surgeon, and the guv. I slipped and stabbed my chest.'

'Can I see the wound?'

'No Barbie. It's kind of right up here.' Jessica gestured to the spot through her sweatshirt.

'Show her.'

'But ...'

'Show her.'

Jessica pulled up her top, keeping her left breast covered and as much of her right breast as possible. There was no sound from the seventy-seven inmates. The prison officers inched closer, unsure if to intervene with the entire wing out of cells.

'Ow. That must have hurt.' Barbie pulled Jessica's top up completely, exposing her to the audience.

Jessica's eyes welled; she felt her teeth lightly chatter.

'It's ok, really.'

'How do you spell your second name?' As Shelly spoke, Barbie lowered Jessica's top, deliberately stroking over her breasts with the back of both hands.

'Khan. K H A N.'

'Really? Not T A Y L O R.'

'No. I think that might have been my mum's maiden name or something.'

'You calling me a liar?'

'No. No, I am just explaining.'

'Time for your lunchtime shower, squeaky-clean totty. Barbie will keep you company.'

'Not today. I had a wash after gym.'

'What are you in for?'

'I don't talk about it. I hit my husband. I thought he was cheating.'

'Here, I'll take your tray back for you.'

'I haven't eaten …'

Barbie leant over, scooping Jessica's portion of jelly with condensed milk into her mouth with her tongue. She collected all four trays and left the table.

Ingrid waited outside Jessica's cell and walked in as Jessica returned.

'Are you on witness protection?'

'No. Of course not.'

Naomi entered the cell, sat cross-legged on the bed, and pointedly stared at the couple.

'But you are using a false name.'

'No! Khan is my name.'

Naomi spoke. 'The Adams were told by the screw that the pig called you Taylor.'

'Not that I remember. There are Taylors on his side of the family. Perhaps he got mixed up. And he is just my cousin.'

'You let them publicly humiliate you. They will find it even easier next time.'

'What? Should I have fought them?'

'There is a middle way, Jess. You could have refused to lift your top without fighting them. Is your switch just on/off?'

'You sound like my husband.'

'Stand up to them, Jess. But don't fight them.'

Naomi shuffled in her place on the bed.

'And you, Naomi, can mind your own business!' Ingrid continued. 'You are Jessica's cellmate, and I am her appointed *insider*. If you go running back to the Adams about this conversation, I will make sure the whole landing knows you are a snitch and gossip. And I will tell the Adams exactly what I have told Jess. If you get a word wrong with your account, they will think you are a liar and a troublemaker.'

'I'm not a snitch!'

'Did your pig purposely use your *other* name, knowing it would get back to the wing?'

'He's just my cousin.'

Chapter Seven

Jessica tried to sleep. She thought about her family, the good times she had with Jason, and even counted sheep. The main radiators heating the communal areas were failing, and the cell heating had shut down completely. The temperature plummeted to less than ten degrees Celsius inside the cells and not much warmer away from the radiators in the shared spaces. The prison issued a set of extra blankets and jumpers.

Inmates began a spree of low-level vandalism, knocking over tables, pulling taps from the wall, and stamping on water pipes, causing them to leak. Officers locked the inmates down as a precaution. Supper was an outside caterer's sandwich, and an apple delivered to the cells. Jessica's food remained undelivered.

Jessica's belly ached and rumbled so badly that even Naomi took pity and gave her a bag of cheddar crackers, on double bubble. Dawn barely penetrated the outside gloom as Jessica watched the freezing rain lash against the draughty window. Fingers of ice grew on the inside of the glass around the leaking steel frame.

Before the kitchen workers were released from cells, the prison officers set steaming pots of tea on the mess tables to greet the prisoners. They piled up sealed pots of catering hot porridge for the prisoners to thaw and to pacify them. *Cooked* breakfast was then served as usual – cold burgers left over from the previous lunch with a fried egg, sandwiched between slices of fried bread. Jessica resisted the urge to gag as congealing oil from the bread ran cold down her throat.

She was too cold to use the gym or shower. Ingrid avoided her within sight of the Adams. Jessica returned to her cell to put on her remaining clothes and wrap herself in blankets. Still tired from the sleepless night, she lay still listening to the sleet thrash against the window.

Ingrid stepped into the cell again, speaking in a whisper.

'Jess. Have you seen the flyer?'

Jessica sat in her bunk, shaking the fug from her head.

'What flyer?'

'There is a news report of your bail and remand hearing doing the rounds. A photocopy of a *Portsmouth News* court roundup article. Says there are reporting restrictions and a witness's name is redacted from the court summary.'

'It can't be mine!'

'Under the name of *Taylor*. The name your *cousin* used in front of a screw.'

'Shit.'

'The Adams have a conspiracy theory. They are saying you are an MI6 agent.'

'Of course I'm not. That is ridiculous.'

'They have some information from outside, from the dark web.'

'About me? Rubbish.'

'It links you with naval intelligence and Kurdish separatists.'

'Bollocks, Ingrid. I work for Company in the naval base, flogging guns and military hardware. Company is the largest engineering employer in Portsmouth. I'm not a spy! I just sell guns and stuff. Half this lot inside will know someone who works for Company.'

'They think you are a plant or using your position to get your sentence commuted to *suspended.*'

'Honestly, Ingrid, that is all rubbish. And why would they spy on this group of washed-up slags?'

'A related article in the *News* says you tried to kill your husband and his girlfriend.'

'I did not try to kill anyone. And they weren't even seeing each other. It is a storm in a teacup. And what? Don't we like *crims* in nick anymore?'

'It says she was pregnant.'

'Shit, shit, shit.'

'I am not your friend, Jess, and I want you to keep your distance from me. I am telling the senior screw to appoint you a new *Insider*; I quit. My last piece of advice is to get transferred off the wing. The Adams think you are a baby killing nonce and snitching to the filth. Soon they will have the entire wing on their side; I've warned you how hysteria spreads like wildfire. Supporting the Adams to kick shit out of you gets them off everyone else's back and provides some entertainment. Get a transfer.'

'Oh, cosy, cosy.' Shelly spoke as the cell filled with her, Natasha, Barbie, and Naomi.'

'Don't start on me, Shelly. I am her *Insider*. Or I was, I just quit.'

'But you are still on the baby-killer's side.'

'Actually, I am on nobody's side. Not hers and certainly not yours. For what it's worth, I have warned her about the photocopy.' Ingrid held her chin high and blagged confidence, but she rang her hands together behind her back with nerves. 'You don't scare me with your kangaroo courts. If you touch me for being an *Insider*, the governor will be all over you like a rash. They will splinter your little love triangle to the far corners of the kingdom. Now get out of my way.' Ingrid barged past Naomi, the path of least resistance, and left the cell.

'Listen to Miss Snooty.' Natasha spoke to Jessica as if they were old friends, rolling her eyes towards the departing Ingrid. 'You soon learn who your friends are.' She turned her attention back to Jessica. 'You will understand, Mrs Taylor, how we all want to live in harmony and peace. We are big on family values. We can't just ignore things like this. Don't you agree?' She waved two sheets of A4 photocopy paper for effect.

'I haven't seen the articles yet, but they sound ill-informed.'

'Ill-informed, you say? Well, anyway. We don't want informers and baby killers as neighbours, now do we?'

Jessica felt her face burning. Her escape path to the cell door remained blocked, and Naomi stood guard over the alarm; not that the screws would answer it promptly.

'No. Of course. I don't know what the report says. But I am no informer, nor would I ever hurt a baby, obviously. I just kicked out at my husband, mostly. I am not proud, but I am no monster.'

'Would you like some time to digest this information?' She waved the sheets of paper again.

'Yes, please.'

'Shelly love, Mrs Taylor would like to digest these.'

In a moment, Shelly and Barbie were on Jessica. Shelly punched her in the solar plexus as Barbie yanked back her hair until she was looking up at the ceiling. Snatching the paper from Natasha, Shelly rammed it into Jessica's mouth. Jessica tried to bite down on Shelly's fingers, but the paper filled her mouth. Shelly continued to force the paper further down her throat until her mouth was full. Jessica fell to the floor gagging and heaving for breath as Natasha kicked her several times in the abdomen.

'We will pop back to discuss this situation once you have had time to digest it properly. Use that time wisely, Mrs Taylor. I hate to agree with that tree-hugging *Insider* of yours, but I also suggest you get yourself transferred before we meet again.'

Naomi returned to her bunk as the Adams left the cell. Jessica spat out the sheets of photocopy and sat heaving for breath. Each breath hurt her stomach and chest.

'Looks like I will get my cell back to myself. Either the guv will move you to the protection wing, or the hospital wing will collect you on a stretcher. Either way, I won't have to listen to you snivelling all night.'

'You really are all heart, Naomi. I am not transferring to the nonce's wing. I have done nothing to deserve that.'

Naomi shrugged. 'Doesn't bother me. I just hope Shelly doesn't spray your blood over my stuff. Actually, I had better keep it all safe.' She packed her few possessions away into her locker.

Jessica found her phonecard from hidden under the bottom shelf of her own locker and joined the short queue for the payphone. Other inmates pushed in front of Jessica; the officer monitoring the queue did not intervene and Jessica only got to the front when the dinner bell sounded and nobody new joined. She entered her PIN and tapped her solicitor's number.

'Jax, a group of prisoners has threatened me; they know who I am and about Priti's baby. My cousin used my name in front of a screw.'

'A serious threat?'

'Defo. The entire wing knows. They can't back down now.'

'I will put in an urgent request to the governor. You must also put in a request to the senior wing officer.

'Your cousin's name is now removed from the visitor's list. Do you have anything to tell me, Jess?'

'Nothing.'

'Special Branch has also written to the Crown Prosecution Service to flag concerns of national security, relating to incidents involving you in India and Turkey.'

'What incidents?'

'They have not disclosed the details. Can you enlighten me?'

'I visited Turkey during the military coup and got arrested; I left a bit smartish. Kurds also targeted me when I worked in Turkey for my employer, Company. But I absolutely am not a threat. They interviewed me, here in the UK, with no action taken. Is this to stop me from getting bail?'

'Why would Special Branch want to stop bail?'

'Jax, I don't want a transfer to the protection wing. I'm not spending time with the scum on protection.'

'I might get you isolated, perhaps on your current wing.'

'No! They can't lock me up all day. I am claustrophobic.'

'Hopefully only until bail.'

'It doesn't work like that, Jax. I have panic attacks when they lockdown at night, and that is when I am not alone, and I know when they will open the door in the morning. No Jax. I will take my chances here.'

'I will talk to the prison management. Perhaps they will have a suggestion. Put your request in without delay.'

Jessica walked past the prisoners eating and collecting their lunches. They all hissed as she passed. Concentrating on looking directly ahead, she continued to the office, standing facing the closed door. An officer approached her.'

'Not hungry today, Khan? Or is it Taylor? I lose track.'

'May I talk to the Senior, please, Miss?'

'Why?'

'I need a transfer, Miss.'

'Why? Don't you like it here?'

'I love it here, Miss. But *it* doesn't love me.'

'Have you been threatened?'

'Yes, Miss.'

'By whom?'

'I can't remember, Miss. But I believe I will be attacked soon. Ask my *Insider*, Miss. She heard the same rumour.'

'Ok, Khan. Go and have your lunch. I will arrange a meeting with the Senior Officer. Is your cellmate a threat?'

'Not specifically, Miss.'

'Ok. Off you go.'

The food queue fell silent as Jessica joined the back. The server refused to slop Jessica's food onto her tray, saying they had run out. Jessica used her plastic spoon to load mashed potato, peas, boiled chicken, and runny gravy onto her own tray.

As she walked past the rest of the queue collecting biscuits and ice cream, an inmate turned to Jessica and spat. It missed the food but splattered against Jessica's hand. Jessica glared at the woman and over at the inactive officer. As she continued to her seat, the remaining queue spat as she passed, landing on her food and chest.

'You can't sit here, Jess. I told you.'

'There isn't anywhere else, Ingrid. I have asked for a transfer. This is the last mealtime you will have to sit with me.'

Jessica used the handle of her spoon to push spit and snot to the side of her tray. She had forgotten to collect a plastic knife and fork, so used her fingers to pick up a gravy covered piece of chicken, taking a bite. As soon as the pasty chicken and weak gravy touched her tongue, her belly let out a deep rumble.

'Fuck off Jess.'

'No Ingrid, you fuck off.'

Ingrid stood, leant over the table, and tipped Jessica's tray into her lap. The remaining chicken fell to the floor.

Jessica stood, tensing her fists. Both women knew Jessica had no fight in her and was too scared of her environment to take a swing.

'No Jess, you fuck off.'

Scared and humiliated, tears poured down Jessica's cheeks. The prisoners erupted into applause, stamping their feet, and banging the tables. Officers moved into a line facing the inmates. The Senior Officer approached Jessica.

'Khan, I think it is best you return to your cell. I will take you to the governor once we lockdown following lunch.'

'Boss.'

Jessica returned to her cell with laughter ringing in her ears.

Naomi returned to the cell, with a few minutes of lunch association left to run.

'Why do you stare at the window, Jess? You can't see anything.'

Jessica shrugged. 'Has anyone ever escaped? Is there an escape committee?'

Naomi giggled into her pillow.

'This isn't The Great Escape. You dumb bitch. But, apparently, rumour has it, there is a door leading from the wing office to the adjacent unused wing. It is an escape route if any officer is trapped in the office during a riot. But if you got into the old wing, it is still secure. So, you are no better off. Try hiding in the laundry trolley, dumb fuck.'

'You really are a nasty cow, Naomi.'

'Make sure you get me my replacement Cheddars before you transfer. Jacobs.'

'Hi ladies!' The Adams entered the cell. Natasha continued. 'Still here Mrs Taylor? A bit risky, don't you think?'

'I'm waiting to meet the guv. I think they will move me today. I really don't deserve this, Natasha. Honest.'

'Let's have a nice cuppa, Jess. Hear your side of the story.'

Jessica took her small travel kettle from her box and topped it with water from the toilet bottle. It only held enough for two cups, but Jessica only had her one tin mug in the cell.

'Sure. I slapped this girl who had been chasing my husband. I found her in my house. But I don't think she was pregnant. They haven't given me the details yet. I think maybe there was a baby, but maybe she already had an abortion or something. I am not sure. But I didn't kill any baby. *The Portsmouth News* has the wrong end of the stick.'

Jessica retrieved her mug, tea bag, and bag of sugar from her locker, placing the items on the table under her top bunk. Her hands shook.

'Shame you must go, Jess. You are a pretty thing to have around. Barbie has a bit of a crush on you. Perhaps you two would like a moment alone? You would have a pleasant memory to take with you.'

Jessica's heart pounded. She knew she was blushing and shaking. She shook her head slightly. 'No. Thank you.'

'Barbie not pretty enough, for you?'

'It's not that.' Jessica tried to speak confidently, but she sounded scared. 'Barbie is pretty. But I am married and everything.'

Natasha laughed. 'I am only messing, Jess.'

Jessica forced a smile.

'Anyway, Jess. We have another idea for a reminder of us to take with you.'

Jessica nodded slowly.

'Which hand did you use to punch that poor mum in the stomach? Are you right-handed?'

'I kicked …'

'Speak up Jess!'

Jessica cleared her throat. 'I kicked her. But I didn't know she was pregnant. I don't think she was actually pregnant.'

'Which foot Jess?'

'I think my right foot kicked her face. I think my left foot kicked her stomach.'

'Well, we can't blame you for kicking the slut in the face, what with her fucking your husband and everything.'

Jessica shrugged.

'But you shouldn't have kicked a pregnant girl in the belly.'

Jessica nodded.

'Is she prettier than you?'

Jessica nodded.

'And I bet she is younger.'

Jessica nodded again.

'Always the way, Jess. Is she a better fuck, do you think?'

Jessica shrugged. 'Maybe.'

Outside, the whistle blew, to announce the lunchtime association would end in ten minutes. The kettle boiled and clicked off.

'Give Jess a goodbye kiss, Barbie. We won't see her again.'

Jessica screwed her eyes closed. Her teeth chattered. Barbie moved behind Jessica, slid her hand up Jessica's top, squeezing her bare breasts. She sucked Jessica's earlobe into her mouth and slid her tongue into her ear. Bile rose in Jessica's throat. Barbie slipped her free hand over Jessica's mouth.

'Anyway Jess. Before we return to our little bungalow, we will leave you our little reminder. You will never forget us, and you will never forget which foot you used to stamp an unborn baby to death.'

Jessica opened her eyes wide as Barbie clamped her hand harder around Jessica's mouth and painfully grabbed a handful of Jessica's breast. Natasha lifted Jessica's left leg from under her calf, forcing her further back against Barbie.

'And if we ever see you again, we will match your face with your foot.'

Shelly pulled off Jessica's shoe and sock, throwing them into the toilet bucket. She clicked the kettle on again and poured in the bag of sugar. Jessica twisted, thrashed, and kicked, but the two women easily restrained her, off balance. She screamed into Barbie's hand. Shelly slowly poured the sticky, boiling sugar-water over her restrained foot.

Jessica lay on the floor, unable to touch her burnt foot, screaming in pain. Once the Adams had left the cell, Naomi hit the alarm and poured cold water over Jessica's foot until help arrived.

Chapter Eight

Jessica sat on the edge of her bed, her bandaged foot resting on a foot stall, wrapped with a cold compression. Iodine stained her calf and shin above the bandage line.

'What have we here, doctor?'

'A nasty burn, governor. Once the swelling has died down, we will need a proper assessment. I am guessing one or more skin grafts.'

'Muscle damage?'

'Too early to say. Naomi is our reluctant hero. She applied cooling water within the crucial time.'

'What happened, Khan?'

'I was making a cup of tea and slipped, guv.'

'With a kettle full of sugar?'

'Ok governor, that is enough,' interjected Mrs Wilson. 'We all know my client was attacked. We asked for a transfer off the wing. HMP Kingston has let down my client - badly. We all know her vulnerability, because of inaccurate information being spread around by your officers.'

'A serious allegation, Mrs Wilson. Choose your words carefully.'

'I will talk to my client further, regarding naming names, but for now we need to discuss her safety going forward.'

'And that is why we are here, Mrs Wilson. Busy as we all are. We will move you onto the protection wing,

Khan. We are better geared to stop the inmates from ripping each other apart on the protection wing.'

'I can't go onto the protection wing, guv, please. I am not a paedophile.'

'Neither can you go back to the main wing, Khan.'

'I can't go onto the protection wing, guv. I'll kill myself.'

The chaplain spoke from her seat next to the prison surgeon. 'Hey, Jessica. Calm down. Nobody is going to kill anyone. Not even themselves. We will find a way. You said you are claustrophobic?'

Jessica bowed her head and spoke to her bandaged foot. 'I just kicked a girl. I didn't mean for any of this to happen.'

The chaplain rubbed her own belly. Approaching full term herself, she had agreed to come into work from maternity leave for this meeting. 'May I ask about transferring her to a different prison, governor?'

'We can look at that chaplain, but it takes time to arrange and there are budget implications.'

'Can I stay here in the hospital wing until then, please guv?'

'That is a no Khan. You are perfectly well enough to return to the wing on light duties.'

'This shithole is massive. There must be other wings, guv, please.'

'Most of this *shithole* is shutdown, Khan. HMP Kingston will be luxury flats within a few years. Oh, the irony. There is the closed wing you were on. We have the hospice/care wing with a couple of lifers at end of life. We have the protection wing, which you know about. And we have the restricted wing.'

'The restricted wing?'

'Category A, maximum security, Mrs Wilson. We have half a handful of guests who pose a high risk of absconding and are a risk to national security. I am not sure your client kicking her husband and his friend qualifies for a place on that wing, not even if your client is clumsy when making a cup of tea.'

'Can't I get a transfer to an open prison? Everyone here knows I am not really an absconding risk.'

'All remand prisoners are held in closed prisons, Jess. But going back to your earlier point, governor, you realise my client is flagged as a threat to national security?'

'Really?' The governor could not hide her surprise.

'Special Branch put a flag on the police file. The prosecution will raise it at the bail hearing.'

'Not my problem, but I expect someone will mention it to me, if the court accepts the argument.'

'I am mentioning it now, governor.'

'Meaning what, Mrs Wilson?'

'Meaning my vote is you move my client to the restricted wing with the other security risks. You can keep her safe and allow free association.' Mrs Wilson raised her hand to show her vote.

The governor looked around the room, the chaplain and surgeon raised their hands to support Mrs Wilson's suggestion.

'Put your hand down, Khan. Nobody is asking for your opinion.'

The guards pushed Jessica on to the maximum-security restricted wing in a wheelchair. Compared to the closed wing, the restricted wing felt calm and clean. High mesh fences split the lower landing in two. Similarly, gates and fences closed off the stairs, creating a small corridor of eight cells in two rows of four. Six cells stayed locked closed, with two cells opposite each other remaining open. The officer pushed Jessica to the open door of one cell.

A young woman of South Asian heritage approached Jessica, leaving two others sat on low sofas around an electric fan heater. She helped Jessica out of the wheelchair, into the cell and down onto her bed.

'Thank you. It is very sore to touch, but it isn't too bad to walk on. My name is Jessica. I am sorry to crash your cell.'

'Hi, I am Alisha. I'm glad to have a roommate; it gets lonely on my own. The screws get funny if we go into each other's cells. But when you are ready, I will help you walk over to the others.'

'How many of us are there?'

'Four, including you. You can see Bashira through the door, the big girl. Shamima is sitting with her back to us. The heating isn't working properly, so we are huddling around a fan heater.'

'It is so clean here, compared to the other wing.'

'That's Shamima. She gets us to clean for an hour every day.'

With Alisha taking her arm, Jessica hobbled to the other women and plonked herself on the third sofa. Alisha sat next to Jessica, still holding her arm.

'Welcome. Who have we here? What happened to your foot?'

'Thank you. I am Jessica Khan. I spilt tea over my foot.'

'My name is Shamima. Let's try all of that again, shall we?'

Jessica felt herself blush, looking at her bandaged foot for inspiration.

'Um. Ok. So, my married name is Taylor. But I was processed using my maiden name.'

'Indian?'

'Afghani on my grandfather's side.'

'The foot?'

'I was punished.'

'For?'

'For something I didn't do.'

'And what didn't you do?'

Jessica lowered her voice further until she was barely audible over the fan heater.

'I kicked a girl who I thought was fucking my husband.'

'Was she?'

'Apparently not.'

'That it?'

'She was pregnant.'

'Was?'

Jessica nodded. 'I didn't know she was.'

'Now tell me something I don't know, Jessica Taylor nee Khan.'

Jessica looked between the three women. Alisha smiled, giving Jessica's arm a reassuring squeeze.

'Special Branch is on to me. They class me as a national security risk.'

'And are you?'

Jessica raised her head to study her interrogator, realising Shamima was the decision maker Dolly wanted her close to.

'Maybe.'

'What happened?'

'I gave some Syrian Kurds information about a NATO product I was working on.'

'Are you Muslim, sister?'

Jessica shrugged. 'I am actually a bit lost. I want to use my time inside to study, prepare, and convert.'

'Convert from?'

'From my emptiness.'

'Fancy a curry pot-noodle'

'Double bubble?'

The three women laughed.

'No sister, you are home now.'

The guards delivered the remains of Jessica's belongings; everything of any value already stolen. Alisha offered to wash Jessica's remaining clothes and underwear in the prisoner washing machine. She also leant Jessica fleece lined walking leggings and a heavy fleece jumper. Jessica snuggled under her blankets.

'I washed and dried your blankets, as well. They were already cleaned but smelt musty. I'll show you where everything is later. We are self-contained here; zero contact with any other inmates. There is a tiny kitchen, and we do our own cooking and washing. Shamima has food sent in, and we club together to buy supplies from the shop each Friday. Are you in with all that?'

'God yes. And the cleaning. I could scrub both cells sliding around on my bum until my foot is a bit better. I can scrub the toilets and everything.'

Seeing Jessica fighting back tears, Alisha hugged her close.

'I'm sorry Alisha. I never used to cry. Now I don't stop. My husband calls me Bambi, because the first time he saw me cry was at the Bambi film. I didn't mean to kill the baby, honestly.'

'Allah will judge you, Jessica, not me. Only Allah gives life, and only Allah should take a life. If you have made a genuine mistake, it is from Allah you must beg forgiveness, not me.'

Jessica nodded, sniffing. Alisha leant forward, kissing Jessica's forehead.

Jessica woke screaming. She had climbed out of bed asleep, landing heavily on her damaged foot, adding pain to her confusion. She pressed the alarm. Alisha pulled her away and, hugging her, pulled her back into the corner, away from the door. The door opened, two male and one female officer burst into the cell. Alisha spoke loudly, confidently, but calmly.

'Sorry, boss. She is sleepwalking. Everything is ok, boss. I've got this.'

The lights now glared brightly. Jessica blinked at her surroundings. Alisha settled a trembling Jessica back into bed. Adding her own blankets, Alisha climbed into bed with Jessica, cuddling her from behind and soothing Jessica's shakes.

'Do you still love your husband?'

'Very much Alisha. But it is over between us.'

'I am sorry to hear that.' There was a brief pause before Alisha continued in a low, soothing tone. 'I have a boyfriend.'

'Really? Wow! You must miss him.'

'He's in here. He's a screw.'

'No! What? Is that even allowed?'

'They can't stop people from falling in love. We haven't, you know, done it or anything.'

'Is he on this wing?'

'Yeah, sometimes. That is how we met. Obviously.'

'Will I meet him?'

'Yeah. I hope so. He has heard we are moving soon. They do that. They don't trust their own people, so they move us on as soon as we have settled in.'

'Can I ask why you are here?'

Jessica felt Alisha's shoulders shrug against her back.

'Bashira and I were involved in recruiting girls to work for Islamic State, ISIL. Silly really. I just wanted to help with the struggle. Shamima was on the news. She is an ISIL bride. She is stateless now and might be extradited to Bangladesh or even back to Syria to face trial.'

'Is she in charge? In here, I mean.'

'Yeah. She is as good as gold, but she was an ISIL enforcer, not one to mess with. We all have to attend de-radicalisation courses to stand any chance of parole. If anything, Shamima is radicalising the team sent to de-radicalise us. Ironic really. The Imam involved runs messages to her people on the outside. Anyway, ask her yourself. I shouldn't be gossiping.'

'Is ISIL operating in the UK?'

Alisha shrugged again against Jessica's back.

'Shamima is involved with the Islamic Forum of Europe now. Ask her, she will tell you what she feels is appropriate. Let's get some sleep.'

Alisha snuggled her nose and mouth into the nape of Jessica's neck. For the first time since entering prison, Jessica felt warm and a little less alone.

Jessica woke to snow piling up against the high window. Alisha sat on her own bed, watching Jessica wake. She had one blanket around her shoulders, leaving Jessica snug under three blankets.

'You are so pretty when you sleep. Not a care in the world; totally relaxed.'

Jessica yawned and stretched, smiling back at Alisha.

Alisha continued. 'I've boiled water and scrubbed my hands. Let's get this done and dusted.'

She had Jessica's ointments and clean dressings laid out over her own bed.

'No Alisha. Thank you, but no. I can't bear the thought of anyone near my foot. And it will turn you off your breakfast.'

'Don't be such a baby.'

She slid over a plastic desk chair, covered with clean paper towels, for Jessica to rest her foot. Jessica covered her head with her hands, screwing closed her eyes in anticipation of the pain. Alisha gently, but firmly, removed the old dressing and gauze. Pulling away the gauze felt like having her foot sandpapered but was less sharp and painful than Jessica expected. Alisha dabbed the wound with the boiled and cooled water, gently drying the foot with a sterile pad. She applied ointment using her bare hands. Jessica felt a tightening of the skin, but her touch was soothing. Alisha sung a traditional Bangladeshi lullaby as she wrapped Jessica's foot in fresh gauze and bandage.

'There, done. That wasn't so bad, was it?' Holding her hands clear, like a surgeon, Alisha leant over and gave Jessica a long kiss on the mouth. 'That's for being a brave girl.'

Jessica covered her face with both hands, blushing deeply, but beaming back at her new friend.

'We associate for breakfast, lunch, and evening. I will walk in the yard with the others, but I think you need to keep that foot dry and warm for a couple of days.'

It was Bashira's turn to cook breakfast, but Jessica asked to be allowed. She poached eggs in salted water, preparing her own version of eggs benedict, using lightly toasted white bread instead of muffins. She heavily peppered salad cream from an out-of-date bottle in the fridge, instead of hollandaise. Jessica also prepared an extra portion for the young prison officer stood to one side of the kitchen. Standing with his back to the CCTV camera, he ate his surprise breakfast in a couple of mouthfuls.

The guard retired back against a closed cell door, out of sight of the CCTV. Alisha joined him. The couple stood leaning back against the door, arms touching.

'Tell me more about your Kurdish connection.'

Jessica intended to sidle up to Shamima as much as possible in case DC Dolly insisted on holding her hostage to his fortune. Whatever she had done in the past, Shamima was now safely off the streets. Under the circumstances, Jessica felt she was the last person who should judge Shamima, especially following the compassion and understanding she had shown Jessica.

'I was working on an anti-aircraft system in Turkey. Kurdish Peshmerga fighters kidnapped me, and I worked with them for a bit.'

Although Jessica had not sided with the Kurdish fighters, she had developed ties with them. She kept her story as factually accurate as possible in case Shamima was able to have Jessica researched.

'And you are still in contact with the Kurds?'

'No, not at the moment. British marines attacked the unit of Kurds holding me. They released me and killed, well, murdered my contact.'

'I cannot decide if you are a willing ally of the Kurdish separatists or a reluctant victim.'

Jessica held Shamima's eye. 'I am not always sure myself. But I believe the Kurdish struggle is right and just. If I ever get out of here, I might offer them my support again. There is little left for me from my old life.'

'Your Kurds fought ISIL.'

'They did.'

Shamima scoffed.

'And you had a meeting with Special Branch or MI6 here, in prison.'

Jessica could not see any advantage in lying. She nodded. 'Yes, Special Branch, I think. They have flagged me as a threat to national security.'

'Who did you see?'

'He didn't give me his name. He told the prison he was my cousin, Parton. But I don't have a cousin called Parton.'

'And the fight?'

'How do you know all this, Shamima?'

Shamima glanced at the young prison officer talking to Alisha, and back to Jessica.

'Ok Shamima, that was a genuine coincidence. I wasn't feeling brilliant. When I realised it wasn't really my cousin, I stood to storm out but tripped or fainted and fell on my chair.'

'And injured?'

'Not really.' Jessica lifted her top to show the almost healed puncture wound, caused by the surgical tool wielded by PC Dolly.

'What did he ask of you?'

'Nothing. He didn't have a chance. As soon as he walked in, I stormed out. But when I was working in India recently, I accidentally overdosed on malaria medication. I don't like to talk about my mental health, but at best it is fragile. With the Chloroquine overdose and my paranoia, I hallucinated I was being stalked by my Kurdish contact.'

'The dead one?'

'Don't take the piss, Shamima.'

'I am not, Jessica. Please continue.'

'Anyway, the Indian Police Service got involved. They informed Special Branch, who confiscated my husband's laptop. I assume this Parton bloke wanted to talk about that incident. I had only just landed in the UK when the *domestic* happened, and I was arrested.'

'You have heard the expression *my enemy's enemy*.'

'Yes, of course. *Amicus meus, inimicus inimici mei. My friend, the enemy of my enemy.*'

'And you Jess. Are you my friend?'

'We certainly share the same enemies.' Jessica gestured to the surrounding prison.

Shamima maintained eye contact, slowly nodding. Alisha flopped into the seat next to Jessica.

'Apparently you have a bail hearing, Jess?'

'Yes. Tomorrow.'

'No, this afternoon.'

'No Alisha, tomorrow, Tuesday. Today is a bank holiday.'

'Today is Tuesday.'

'Shit!'

'We submitted your bail application. The magistrates did not see the need to call you to court, but I fought your corner. We made a big deal about your having been injured and the police inertia to charge you with any crime. Special Branch has refused to remove the flag regarding national security, but also refuses to expand on the reasons.'

'Bottom line, Jax?'

'You are remanded for another seven days. Wait Jess, calm down. The magistrates are losing patience. I believe they will release you on bail at the end of this seven-day period if the police have not shown a significant move towards charging you. Is this wing any better?'

'Yes.' Jessica's chest heaved, but she remained calm. 'The other cons are much more civilised. They seem to accept my version of the assault without drama.'

'My advice is still to keep your distance. I understand Shamima is on this wing. She is a serious criminal with blood on her hands. She is also dangerously persuasive. Think God fearing Hannibal Lecter. And if there is one thing I know about you Jess – you are impetuous and easily led.'

'She is actually ok, Jax. I guess we all do as she tells us. But she is fair enough, and the atmosphere is much less wild west.'

'No, Jess. She is not fair, and she is not ok. I have warned you.'

'The thing is Jax, I have been told they are planning something.'

'You *have been told*? Told by whom? By Shamima?'

Jessica shook her head. 'I shouldn't say.'

'Don't tell me DC Dolly Williamson!'

Jessica shrugged.

'What is going on, Jess?'

'He just mentioned that he could influence the police investigation if I report back on Shamima.'

'What? In those exact words?'

'Not exactly, Jax. But that is what he was getting at.'

'You are playing with fire, Jess.'

'He said that.'

'I don't mean breaking rules Jess, I mean losing your life!'

'He said that as well. But what have I got to lose?'

'Your bloody life, Jess. That is what you have to lose! You know I can't represent you on this. All I can do is to advise and represent you in court regarding

109

any charges. I'm not playing cloak and dagger with your safety.'

'I know, I am just saying. I have nobody else to tell. I don't trust DC Dolly. It was him who leaked my married name.' She gestured towards her bandaged foot. 'He first raised the idea of my coming onto the restricted wing. No doubt he had me flagged as a national security risk, to make sure the governor had the authority to transfer me here; realising the others would target me. But, honestly Jax, what would you do? Spend twenty years inside and risk extradition on release? Or shadow someone for a week with the promise of a second chance at the end of it?'

'I wouldn't have kicked my husband and his friend in the first place!'

'That is less than helpful, Jax.'

'What can you possibly learn in a week that is so important to Special Branch? My advice is to trust in the process and mitigate the situation through the courts.'

Jessica snorted a sardonic laugh. 'Yeah, ain't that approach working just dandy? He just said stay close wherever it takes me.'

'We know where it will take you, Jess – to a week sharing a prison with Shamima. Nowhere else! I have tapped-up the prosecutor for any gossip. He doesn't think Special Branch has any interest in the actual assault. Don't make things more complicated, Jess.'

The women were locked down for the night when Jessica was escorted back to her cell. Inside felt warm, with the senior officer agreeing the prisoners could take the fan heater into their cells on alternate nights; cutting the electric cord to just a couple of inches long. Alisha lay under her blankets as Jessica brushed her teeth in the handbasin and slid into bed. She wanted to share Alisha's body heat, comfort, and blankets. With the heater whirring away, she could think of no justification to make that suggestion.

'Bail didn't go well?'

'Not really. My brief thinks I will stay on remand through to court and sentencing,' Jessica lied.

'I am really sorry to hear that, Jess. But we get to keep you a bit longer.'

Jessica smiled at the sentiment. 'Your chap is real eye-candy Alisha.'

'Thank you. I am so in love. I am not stupid, though. It can't last.'

Jessica was unsure how to respond – it hardly being a match made in heaven.

'He told me something today. I shouldn't tell anyone, but it will affect you.'

'Go on.'

'I have told Shamima. Please don't tell her I told you.'

'Sure. Go on.'

'They are going to move us all in a few days.'

Jessica's heart leapt. If they move Shamima away, DC Dolly would have to accept Jessica could no longer spy on her. Hopefully, he would release her from their *contract*, allowing Jessica and Mrs Wilson to concentrate on answering any charges for the assault.

'Oh no! I am really going to miss you guys. As I am only on remand, they won't move me. I bet the next inmates won't be as cool as you three.'

'My chap is preparing to take six men associated with the English Defence League.'

'Men? But we are a woman's nick!'

'The closed and restricted wings are women-only. The hospice wing is mixed, and this wing is either/or.'

'Where will we go? I will have to tell my brief.'

'No Jess, please. You will get me in trouble with Shamima and my chap might also get into trouble. We will know where we are going, once we get there. He thinks it might be Bronzefield in Ashford. A privately owned dump where the screws let sick women choke to death on their own vomit. They will probably keep us together or incarcerated with other Islamists. They won't let us mix with other cons. You will be ok Jess. I will keep an eye on you.'

Jessica screwed her eyes shut, concentrating on calming the rage and fear rising in her chest.

Guards took the other three women through the heavy barred fence leading to the unused half of the landing. Jessica saw them in the distance, sat in a circle with an Imam and an outer circle of four prison officers. She could now stand on her injured foot for short periods, so cleaned her cell. As an excuse, she also cleaned the other women's cell, checking for anything she thought might interest DC Dolly. The women had a copy of the Quran wrapped in a patterned gold coloured fabric. They neatly stowed worry beads and prayer mats on a separate shelf, along with a small pad of yellow rice paper. Like her own cell, they also kept a lota and a plastic curtain to drape over the toilet when eating or praying, but nothing of interest to Jessica or DC Dolly.

Jessica cleaned the small kitchen area, hoping to ingratiate herself still further with the others. She would make a point of learning the bathroom etiquette, remembering she had to enter on one foot, leave on another, and face towards Mecca at some point. At least the good Muslim girls did not talk or stare when in the shared bathroom, or when Jessica needed to use the cell toilet.

With Jessica deep in thought, the officer made her jump and yelp, talking over her shoulder. She apologised and laughed.

'Sorry boss. I was miles away, or at least I wish I was.'

He smiled back.

'Thank you for the egg the other day. I have a little present for Alisha. And you guys, obviously.' He slid a large slab of cheese under a tea-towel, folded onto the counter. Jessica did not acknowledge the present, moving it to the fridge away from the CCTV. The

113

officer took his usual position leant against one of the closed cell doors.

By the time the three convicts returned from their de-radicalisation class, Jessica had made a steaming dish of pasta bake. She used a small tin of tuna, various leftover shapes of dried pasta from an old biscuit tin, a tiny tin of peas and a generous portion of the cheese. She crushed in her own bag of cheese and onion crisps into the sauce, to give it some crunch.

Bashira hardly spoke to the other inmates, and never to Jessica unless asked a direct question. Shamima seldom chitchatted but made a point of engaging the others throughout the day. She had a non-confrontational and endearing way of detailing the others by giving her instructions as if from a third party. Alisha was bubblier and more open, gushing over any slight changes to anyone's hair or makeup. She wore her hijab when meeting with her boyfriend or in formal meetings with the Imam or male officers, but remained uncovered throughout the rest of the day, even if other male officers were on the landing. Jessica followed Alisha's lead, laughing at even the most casual jokes, and offering to help with every task. She wanted to get as close to Shamima as possible so she would have something to keep DC Dolly onside, even if she eventually gained bail before obtaining any significant information. She was burning no bridges with DC Dolly until she had faced charges, unsure of the influence he held.

It also helped pass the time to help the others, and it gave her a warm feeling, especially if Shamima showed any appreciation for something she had done. The women showed Jessica concern and compassion, and Jessica felt less desperate than when on the closed wing. Especially on the alternate nights when the other cell had the fan heater, Jessica lay in bed, longing for Alisha to join her again. That possibility seemed behind them, for now.

'Did you have a main office, Jess?'

'At work Shamima? Yeah, I was based in Company offices in the Portsmouth naval base. Not like my own office or anything, but I would have a desk on which ever floor I was working, depending on the project. Nothing posh or anything.' Jessica had begun her answer with some enthusiasm, but now felt self-conscious discussing her defunct old life.

'A big base?'

'Yes, one of the largest in Europe.'

'Did the security bother you?'

Jessica shrugged. 'Not really, you know? You get used to it.'

'I suppose they already cancelled your passes?'

'Yes, I imagine so. The passes remain the property of the base. They are probably already taking steps to recover them from home. But everything is electronic, so I guess already deactivated.'

'Yeah. Can't have members of the public just wondering around.'

'No. Not really. The public has access to the Historic Dockyard without a pass, but not the working sections. Have you never been to the dockyard?'

'Not really my bag, Jess. And I am not from Portsmouth. I lived in East London, before Syria.'

'But you are interested now?'

Shamima laughed, shaking her head. 'Just chatting Jess. I have spent months *living* in Portsmouth but haven't chatted with a Pompey girl. Don't worry about it.'

'Not a problem, Shamima. I enjoy talking about life outside. This shithole doesn't feel like Pompey to me. I forget where we are sometimes.'

'What is Portsmouth like?'

Alisha joined the women, and without asking permission, brushed Jessica's hair. Bashira cleared away the lunch dishes.

'Probably a bit like East London. The most densely populated city in the country. A bit of a rough diamond. I wasn't born here, and I am probably a little dark to be classified as a Pompey girl, but I like it.'

'Isn't the whole of the naval base *historic*?'

'Yes, I suppose so. But they open one section to the public, which contains some naval heritage.' Jessica noticed how Shamima had brought the conversation back to the dockyard. Pretending not to have noticed, she expanded. 'So, there is HMS Warrior, dead cool. HMS Victory and lots of museums, other boats and ships to see. In the summer, there is quite a festival vibe. Sometimes I just wander down the main drag and eat an ice-cream, just to get out of the office.'

'And the Mary Rose? I bet that is all miles away from the warships?'

'Yes, Mary Rose is in the Historic Dockyard. Just past the Mary Rose is the Queen Elizabeth Aircraft Carrier Docks. You can clearly see the carriers from the public access – but there is an exclusion zone, obviously.'

'Yeah, obviously. I bet you miss it all, Jess. When you get out of here, you will take none of it for granted, ever again.'

'*If* I get out of here, you mean?'

A surprise solitary tear ran down Jessica's cheek and she heaved a deep sigh. Alisha stopped brushing Jessica's hair and folded her arms around her neck and shoulders, squeezing her into a hug.

'Let's dig you a tunnel, Jess. Dig for freedom.'

'Thanks Shamima. I know you would if you could. Hopefully, I will get bail soon, but I am already dreading having to come back in on sentencing. If there was a tunnel, I would take it. I would risk everything for half a chance of absconding.'

'Breaking out of maximum security is pretty much impossible, but that is the easy part compared with staying free. You need a huge and organised backer to achieve that little nugget.'

'I would probably head back to my Kurdish friends in Syria,' Jessica lied, 'and be a Peshmerga fighter. Don't laugh at me, but I fell a bit in love with the woman fighter who kidnapped me. The Brits murdered her, and I miss her. I would rather die in her memory than live in this cage, like an animal.'

'If only we had the chance, Jess?'

'Yeah, if only.'

'Security here must be like that naval base of yours?'

'I wish it was. I wish I knew my way around this lot like I do the naval base.'

'Really? So just for fun, how would you escape from prison, if prison was the historic dockyard.'

'It is all bluster. They concentrate security around the main Victory Gate, and even that is only checking rucksacks to impress the civilian visitors.'

'You could sneak past security, to get in?'

'Probably. I'd pretend I had just come off Southsea beach in a bikini top. I would pick the security queue headed by the youngest, most testosterone dripping MOD Police Officer. Like seriously bad acne.' All three women laughed together. 'But actually, I might pick up the water taxi from the submarine base in Gosport. I would look around HMS Alliance first, then use my ticket to catch the water taxi over to Portsmouth dockyard.'

'But presumably they have similar security at the submarine base?'

'No. There are lots of military labs and establishments in the Haslar complex, but the Alliance is just in a museum area, so no proper security.'

'And the water taxi drops you near the carriers and the Mary Rose? What, like inside the secure zone?'

'If you know your way around, then yes.'

'And you do?'

'And that is only one of the glaring lapses. If they imprisoned me in the naval base, I would have popped up in Kurdistan by now! As you say, *if only*.'

The women laughed again. Jessica dragged her hand across her nose and wet cheeks.

'Was your husband the only man you kissed?'

'God no, Alisha.'

'You probably need to study a bit more before converting, Jess.'

Jessica raised up on her elbows to stare across the gloom of the cell. She could see Alisha's white teeth smiling, topped by the whites of her eyes reflected in the moonlight. The night was the coldest of the winter so far, but at least it was dry and clear with stars freckling the sky. Freezing snow dampened the sound of the few cars which ventured out into the frozen city. Jessica borrowed Alisha's fleece lined leggings and jumper to sleep in. Jessica pulled them on, still warm from Alisha changing out of them. She pulled the top over her face to warm her nose, also smelling the musk of the owner.

'You are probably right there, Alisha. He isn't even the only man I have kissed since marrying him.'

'Jess!'

'None of that seems important anymore. I would do anything to spend a night with Jason now. But to be honest, I would take an airline pilot as second best.'

Jessica had thought of saying a *prison officer*, but the only male on shift today was Alisha's boyfriend.

'An airline pilot? What made you say that?'

'Forget it, Alisha, a long story. It is Friday, date-night. I am just feeling sorry for myself.'

'Tell me about date night.'

'Date nights varied. My favourite was arriving home from work on a wintry day, like this. Jason would have dinner on the go, and a bath ready to share. We'd make love, eat too much curry, drink too much wine, drunkenly try to make love again by the fire, and fall asleep downstairs in front of the telly. Jason would drag me up to bed and when I woke in the morning, I would instigate our love making again, before kicking him out to make coffee.'

'But you don't think he will forgive you for attacking him?'

'No chance. The police believe I actually tried to kill him and an apparently innocent girl. The longer I sit in here thinking about it, the more I doubt myself. Perhaps I *was* trying to kill them.'

'And the baby?'

'No! You mustn't ever think of me like that Alisha, please. Whatever I am found guilty of, I would never hurt a baby. I would die to save a child.'

Alisha slipped out of bed and padded the two steps to give Jessica a hug. Jessica's heart screamed for Alisha to stay with her for the night, but her heart was ignored. Jessica lay in the dark, regulating her breathing to match Alisha's.

Plans swirled and whirred around her head. She would talk to Mrs Wilson, asking to attend the bail hearing on Tuesday, and asking her to get a message to DC Dolly to meet before the hearing. She would tell him about Shamima's interest in the dockyard. Perhaps he would influence the police to remove their objection to bail. Although her mood grew more buoyant since transferring to the restricted wing, she was still anxious. She imagined her plan backfiring and DC Dolly wanting her to stay on remand to find out more from Shamima.

Jessica also ran through plans on how to approach Jason if they released her on bail. Perhaps she could request a meeting through the courts as part of the divorce proceedings. She would beg him to hold off the divorce until after the trial. She would suggest some sort of reparation for Priti. She would assure them both she would admit and agree to anything they wanted. Perhaps she would offer to work with a baby, or mother and baby charity. Jessica would offer to recognise their mutual friendship; Priti could live with them if her parents refused to have her home.

'Jessica, love.'

'Alisha?'

'You are talking to yourself. Get some sleep.'

Chapter Nine

The weekend felt duller and colder, even more so than the previous week. Prison rules banned inmates from having outdoor coats, unless issued and controlled for working in the garden. Jessica received a parcel of warmer clothes, including a heavy, fleece lined jumper from her sister. Despite the cold aggravating her injured foot, she squeezed into her boots to join the other three in the yard. The burn was healing, and the hospital wing now issued a gauze sock each day, to replace the bandaging.

Immediately following breakfast, the three returned to Shamima's cell to talk in hushed voices. Alisha leant against the outside steel doorframe; the other two stood inside the cell. They left Jessica alone to clear the mess table and washup. Washing the dishes as soon as breakfast finished was one of Shamima's rules.

Exercising in the yard, Bashira walked half a step behind Shamima as usual, both in silence. Alisha and Jessica walked together, half a lap behind the others.

'What's the drama, Alisha? Your chap tell you something?'

'After chow? No, nothing, no drama. I slept through sunrise prayers. I feel better telling Shamima that sort of thing.'

'You didn't mention it at breakfast. Your chap mention moving again?'

Alisha flicked a look at the other two inmates across the yard.

'No. Nothing like that. When is your bail hearing?'

'Tuesday. Two sleeps. Are you changing the subject?'

'Stop it, Jessica. I have known Bashira since school and Shamima since nick. I don't have to tell you everything I tell them. You will be out of my life on Tuesday, fingers crossed.'

'Sorry. I just care about you.'

The couple linked arms; the snow dusting their clothes.

'I care about you also, Jessica. I hope you get bail, but I will miss you. Let's go in. I've got enough cocoa and a couple of squares of chocolate to make us all a drink. It will be a pleasant surprise for the girls.'

There were four duty officers on the restricted wing. Two unlocked and walked into the yard with the women. One stayed back, watching from the relative shelter of the open door. The fourth remained on the landing. As Alisha suggested, Jessica left the yard at the end of the lap. She walked along the short corridor back to the landing, now realising Alisha had double backed to talk with the other two inmates.

Jessica prepared for the hot chocolate, warming milk in the microwave and adding coffee creamer to make the drinks richer and thicker. The three followed her into the wing. Alisha peeled off to fetch the cocoa powder from her cell. The other two walked directly to Jessica. A prison officer stood within earshot.

Flicking through the limited programs available on the shared television, she settled on a repeat episode of *A Place in the Sun*.

'Bail soon, Jess.'

Jessica held up crossed fingers to show Shamima.

'Obviously, you can't wait to get out of here. But we will miss you. It is dehumanising, don't you think? They tell you where to go, and when. But I guess that is life, generally. We can't always decide to stick together. Sometimes we go our own way. Yes?'

'Yes, I guess so.'

'We can't go home with you on Tuesday, Jessica, can we?'

'No. More's the pity. But, if I even get bail, we might meet again when I come back in, on sentence.' Jessica shuddered, cupping the small jug of hot milk with her chilly hands.

'Our relationship is just beginning, Jess, whether you are inside or out.'

Shamima spoke gently, with a friendly twinkle in her eye, but the words sent a chill down Jessica's spine.

'Sure. I will never forget your kindness.'

'But like I said, sometimes we have to go our own way for a while. Understood?'

'Sure.' Jessica had a hesitancy in her voice. She was unsure of the point Shamima was making.

'Hold that thought, Jess. Nobody likes a hanger-on. Now let's enjoy our cocoa treat from Alisha and watch some escapism on telly, shall we?

Later that Sunday afternoon, the senior wing officer read a curt note from the governor's office. It promised the boiler repairs were now complete and the system would be fully operational within days.

Alisha would not engage in conversation with Jessica. The others had the fan heater, so Jessica kept on her new jumper in bed and fidgeted to keep warm.

'Are you packing up your stuff ready for the move, Alisha?'

'Shamima likes us to keep everything tidy. You should sort your locker at least once every week.'

'You haven't heard more about the move, then?'

'No Jess. I told you. We know when we know.'

'Do you have a *de-rad* class with the Imam tomorrow?'

'No. It's cancelled.'

'Why?'

'Jessica! I don't know everything. Please stop interrogating me.'

Alisha covered the toilet with a plastic shower curtain provided by the chaplain. She then scrubbed her hands, removed her boots, and prepared for prayers. Following prayers, she remained knelt on the prayer mat and hard floor. Occasionally, she looked up towards Mecca and mumbled a few prayers under her breath. The lights flicked twice and, exactly one minute later, extinguished. Alisha took a deep sigh. Jessica could not be sure in the dark, but she suspected Alisha was fighting back tears.

'Fancy some body-heat, Alisha? I could do with comforting.'

Without answering, Alisha hurried to put away her mat and Quran before pulling her blankets from her bed and climbing in with Jessica. Jessica pulled her close, pulling up Alisha's legs so her icy feet warmed against Jessica.

The bed was too narrow for two adults, even though both women were slim, and Jessica had lost more weight over the past two weeks in prison. Jessica woke whenever Alisha turned, but the comfort of a warm human outweighed any interrupted sleep. Jessica woke to Alisha praying.

The wing senior officer approached the prisoners as breakfast-association ended.

'Ok ladies. Today's de-radicalisation class is cancelled. Obviously, you will not be penalised for non-attendance.' Jessica noticed the feigned surprise of her three prison mates. 'And guess why? You are to move establishments today. How exciting for you?'

Alisha's eyes welled, presumably at the thought of losing contact with her boyfriend. Bashira stared at the officer without expression. Shamima spoke.

'May I speak with the Imam, please?'

'No Shamima.'

'Just on the phone, please, boss? You may monitor the call obviously, boss.'

'May I indeed? That is very kind of you. Still no. Write him a letter.'

'It is hugely disrespectful for us to just *not turn up*.'

'We have told him already.'

'You told him we are moving today, boss?'

'I just said so, Shamima.'

'May I speak with the chaplain, please, boss?'

'You will be pleased to hear the chaplain had her baby last night. She might have other things on her mind. What is going on?'

'I just want to pass a message to the Imam, boss. I want him to know we are not disrespecting him. I want him to know we are moving today and not ignoring him.'

'You are now being disrespectful to me, Shamima! I said he knows. That is good enough. We will issue you prison uniform to travel. You may wear extra layers underneath, but nothing over your uniforms. All visits and telephone calls are suspended, from now. Once you reach your destination, you may make one call each from reception. You are locked down from now. You will have sandwiches for lunch and a sweet little picnic for your journey. We really do spoil you. We will also deliver you two cardboard boxes each for your belongings. Everything must fit inside the boxes, with the lid fitted properly. Be ready before 4pm.'

'Sorry Miss, but I have my bail hearing tomorrow, here in Portsmouth. I don't think I can go to Ashford.'

'Who mentioned Ashford, Jessica?'

'Sorry Miss, I thought you said we are moving to Ashford. But wherever it is, I think I should stay here.

I could go into solitary on the closed wing for the one night.'

'Ok ladies, discussion over – as interesting as it was. Back to your cells, please.'

The senior officer marched towards the office as two wing officers approached the cells, ready to lock down the occupants.

'Jess, why did you say Ashford?'

'That is what she said, Shamima. She said *you are moving to Ashford*, or something.'

'Ok Jess, whatever. You understand we may soon part ways? But I will be in touch.'

The rest of the day dragged. Alisha and Jessica tried to concentrate on a jigsaw puzzle cut from an aerial photograph of the prison. Lunch was Gregg's vegetarian sausage rolls, with a paper cup of lukewarm tomato soup, a pleasant change from prison nosh. Both women slipped on the baggy prison joggers and hoodie over their own clothes for extra warmth; the cell was cold, but the sweatbox transport promised to be colder still.

'Shamima primed me to prepare to be separated.'

'Really? That's odd. Perhaps she has heard you are going to another prison. Perhaps they are going to put you into solitary here.'

'Maybe. Does she talk to your chap?'

'No way. He can't stand her. He says she is leading me astray. He is going to ask to visit me in Bronzefield.'

'Really? Wow, I am so pleased for you. He has a point about Shamima. Perhaps you should distance yourself and concentrate on parole.'

'Look who's talking! You are the one talking about working with Shamima and with the Kurds again.'

'Who else would have told her about me going elsewhere?'

'No idea. The only contact I know she has is the Imam. They swap Qurans at the end of each session, with rice paper notes between the pages. That way, they can quickly digest the note, as it were. But the Imam wouldn't know anything about you moving. Unless the chaplain mentioned it to him. Unlikely if she has been busy squeezing out a sprog.'

Transport arrived at 8pm. They took each prisoner down separately, starting with Jessica. She sat alone in the caged section of the converted Mercedes Sprinter, waiting for each of the others to arrive. She remained shackled until the last prisoner sat. The officer then removed each remaining shackle as she backed out of the cage. Alisha moved seats to sit next to Jessica, but Shamima told them all to sit apart. The officer then sat in the rear section, outside of the cage. She handed her cage key back to the prison officer, so that no cage key rode in the vehicle.

The gates from the garage opened, and the van drove into the courtyard, stopping behind the outer gates. They stayed in the courtyard, waiting for an instruction to proceed. Snow piled around them, on the bonnet of the van and in a line on the windscreen wipers. Through the internal bulkhead window, Jessica idly watched as the wipers occasionally swished snow from the windscreen. She shivered with the cold and uncertainty ahead.

The gates opened, and the van sped into the darkness and snow, turning a hard left and falling in behind a police car. They accelerated along the one-way gyratory, heading North and out of the city. Jessica rested her head against the heavy tinted and barred window. She knew this city thoroughfare, heading from Milton and Kingston towards Hilsea, and the bridges leading off England's only city island.

She recognised one of the short side roads, which led from Milton Road to the railway tracks. Once, she dated a boy who lived down the road with his parents. She wondered if he still lived there – he was a mummy's boy. At the end of the sideroad stood a group of workmen, stamping their feet in the cold. There also stood an old yellow British Gas *elephant* tent, and a ribboned-off heavy JCB digger with forward pointing forks.

Through the front windscreen, Jessica saw the police escort hit a sheet of ice stretching across the road from a hosepipe at the roadworks. The Range Rover span one hundred and eighty degrees; crashing sideways into the row of mechanical workshop lockups, which lined the central reservation of the one-way system. The *sweatbox* entered the skid pad as the driver fought to keep the van moving straight. The JCB lurched from the side road, the forks smashing through Jessica's side window. Momentum of the van turned the digger sideways, so the van now pointed across the road at ninety degrees, impaled on the digger's forks.

Jessica screamed and automatically ducked sideways, away from the digger. The digger now shook the van like a dog with a toy. It continued grinding forward, crushing the side of the van and pushing it over. Jessica now hung from her seatbelt. The van engine over revved, filling the cage and rear compartment with exhaust smoke. The mangled van groaned and creaked as the digger continued to crush the underside and peel off the roof with its forks.

The sound was deafening, making Jessica think of two dinosaurs fighting to the death. Spotlights flooded the remains of the cage with light through the smashed windows and holes punctured and torn into the van's shell. The van engine raced louder before finally exploding and falling silent.

All four women released their seatbelts and fell to the side of the upturned van. Blood poured from Bashira's temple. The officer groaned from her seat outside the cage.

'You, screw, keep still, or they will kill you!' screamed Shamima. 'You, Jessica, sit down and wait to be rescued. You two, out now!'

Alisha clambered up the now vertical roof to escape where the upper side of the van had peeled away from the roof section. Bashira helped Alisha, before turning to help Shamima escape. Jessica jostled Bashira to escape next, but Bashira held her down by her shoulders.

'You heard the boss, Jessica. Stay here and wait. Now give me a leg-up.'

'Bashira, you are injured. Your eyes are looking in different directions. Look at me for a moment.'

'Not now Jess.'

Bashira moved to face Jessica front on. One eye was closing, but they aligned perfectly. Jessica gently took hold of Bashira's chin with her left hand and delivered a right hook to her temple. Bashira crumpled and fell back against the roof in a sitting position.

Jessica stood on Bashira's shoulders to reach the hole. As she wriggled through the jagged steel gap, a pair of hands grabbed under her arms, manhandling her over the edge of the van into another set of waiting arms. They picked her up from under her legs and sat her straight on the pillion seat of a scrambler motorbike. The rider roared the wrong way down the one-way system, back towards the prison.

After fifty yards, the rider took a hard left on a zebra crossing. Crossing between the workshops, they sped straight over the return finger of the gyratory, narrowly missing a gritting lorry. They rode along residential backstreets and through a pedestrian gate into Tamworth Park. Jessica heard the wailing of police sirens from the main roads around the park. Crossing the park at breakneck speed, with no lights, Jessica clutched the rider tight around his waist.

The scrambler shot out of the opposite gate, which was earlier removed from the hinges and discarded. Back on side streets, Jessica tried to find her bearings, but could see nothing with the snow pummelling her eyes. They entered Milton Cemetery, which Jessica recognised by the chapel. The rider sped up along the snow-covered central drive, passing the chapel. Gravestones broke the snow, drifting against the graves and obscuring the edges of the drive. Jessica just made out the tracks of the other two scramblers ahead.

The scrambler clipped the Victorian stone edges of the drive, somersaulting the scrambler and passengers. The bike landed first. Menacingly close, the rear wheel spun as the rider landed on top of the bike. Jessica still clutched his waist, his body cushioning hers from the impact. The rider let out a groan as Jessica's momentum forced out his breath. The spinning rear wheel found purchase against a gravestone, flipping the bike, rider, and Jessica into the air.

The bike stalled. Jessica was thrown clear, landing in thick snow on an empty section of grass. The driver lay against a stone cross, body contorted.

Jessica gasped for breath, slowly sitting, checking her body and limbs for damage.

'Are you ok?'

'No. Can you help me sit?' The man spoke with an Eastern European accent.

Jessica saw the angle of his leg, snapped in several places; the jagged edge of his shinbone exposed.

'No. You are injured. You need help. Where is your mobile?'

Jessica found the man's mobile phone in his top pocket, sticky with blood. She powered up the phone. The man's groans grew louder.

'You will need my password. There is a number stored in contacts under *AAA*.'

'No way, pal. I'm phoning 999. Where were you taking me?'

The man moved his head to look directly at Jessica. He flinched with pain.

'You have to tell me, mate. You aren't in any fit state to deliver me there now, are you?'

The man snorted a response.

'Devil's Asshole.'

'Where's that?'

'Somerstown. Do you know Portsmouth?'

'Yeah. A bit. Look, I need to get going before the *feds* arrive.'

'Great idea. Good luck.'

'Good luck to you, as well.'

Jessica tried to kick-start the scrambler, but it lurched forward, still in gear. She stamped down the gears until reaching neutral. The scrambler started, and Jessica continued forward, following the tracks left by the previous bikes.

At a fraction of the speed taken by the previous rider, Jessica crawled along, navigating the quickly disappearing tracks. Back on the side roads of Milton, Jessica continued south; aware she was conspicuously crawling along the empty roads with no crash helmet or lights, in a snow blizzard. She kept the revs low and sneaked close to the low walls and flat fronts of the Victorian terraces. There was a recently exposed gap in the Victorian railings of St James' mental health facility. The hospital compound was huge. Besides the main hospital wings, stood numerous outbuildings in various states of repair. Some buildings were derelict, others still in use.

Jessica could not make out the driveways in the deepening snow and drifts, and the tracks were now obscured in the near darkness. With the idling engine still driving the bike, she walked it around the side of a plant room and into a hedge. A voice broke the darkness. Jessica screamed and leapt backwards, the bike lurching forward into the hedge and stalling.

'Bugger off. You can't stay here. This is my place. Find your own.'

'God yes. No. Look, sorry, I just want to leave my bike. I am not staying.'

'Ok. The others went that way.'

Jessica followed the pointing hand of the shadow.

'Cool. Thanks.'

'No! You can't walk that way. Go towards those lights, then turn right by that big pipe. Go straight – you can see The Meon pub sign in the distance. Be careful Miss, there are some weirdos who live on these grounds. A right psycho lives in that pipe.'

'Ok. Thank you. I will.'

Locally, there was talk of an ever-increasing community of homeless and mentally ill people living rough within the gates of the old Victorian asylum. Following the directions, Jessica could make out the disappearing shape of the driveway and tried to stay towards the centre. The cold bit through her clothes; her injured foot now throbbing.

Each footstep crunched against the freezing snow; the sound dampened by the covering. Shadows moved in her periphery, black and grey against the night. She reached the junction of the drives at the open end of a Victorian brick tunnel. The occupant had featured as a human-interest story on the local news one Christmas. He lived in the disused *pipe*, the end of a disused sewerage system, since *care in the community* was introduced in the early 1980s. The hospital discharged him into the community. He registered the address as *The Pipe, St James' Hospital, Milton, Portsmouth* to enable him to claim benefits. The Post Office allocated *The Pipe* a post code. On the news, he had appeared quite affable. Tonight, he screamed obscenities and threats as Jessica approached. They reduced in volume and severity as Jessica walked away, along the next section of the drive, her heart pounding with fear.

Near the gateway lay the gate, removed and discarded. Jessica slunk into the shadows under an old decaying metal sign declaring *Portsmouth Borough Asylum*. She stripped off her prison hoodie, joggers, long jumper, thick leggings, and boots, standing on the hoodie in the snow. The icy wind and snow ripped at her flesh, exposed except for socks and knickers. A shadow sniggered from just out of sight. Shaking with cold, adrenaline, and fear, she dressed in reverse order. Stretching the black leggings over the grey joggers and her heavy jumper over the hoodie. All that now showed of the prison uniform was the hood.

She continued towards The Meon pub along Meon Road. The residential street bathed her in streetlight as she kept close to the line of parked cars, now mounds of snow. She was the only person outside, on this normally busy street in the most densely populated city in the country. She limped badly. As the adrenaline rush from her escape, the van crash and bike accident subsided, so the pain of her injured foot, the two crashes, and the cold, intensified.

As she passed The Meon pub, a voice spoke from a smoker stood in the doorway for shelter.

'You ok?'

'Fine. Thanks.'

'Hang on, love.' The man stepped forward, firmly gripping her arm. 'What happened?'

'I slipped in the snow. Please let go of my arm.'

'Look, come inside. I will buy you a drink. Warm up and I'll order you an Aqua cab. I'll pay.'

The man pushed open the pub door, still holding Jessica's upper arm. Light, warm air, and chatter rushed over Jessica. She closed her eyes for a moment and took a deep breath, savouring the atmosphere of the smokeless coal fire. The scent mixed with the alcohol breath and fumes of the few customers talking and drinking inside.

'That is very kind. Thank you. But I live just up the road. I am ok.'

'Where do you live?'

'Let go now, please. Don't make me scream.'

Jessica pointedly looked over the man's shoulder at the pub customers.

'Sorry. Be careful. Six dangerous men escaped from Kingston prison tonight, or something. Best get home.'

As he spoke, the blues of a police Land Rover lit the couple. The car crawled along the centre of the empty road. Police officers shone torches along the path and checked for obvious signs of break-ins along the terraces of Victorian houses. Jessica stepped forward, kissing the man lightly on his lips and pulling herself into a hug. The police car passed the couple and continued towards the hospital.

'Thanks again. It is very kind of you to be concerned. I'm fine, goodnight.'

Jessica pulled away, glanced at the rear lights of the police car, and continued her journey in the opposite direction.

Across the junction with Milton Road stood a lone community police officer, guarding the gates to Milton Park. The gates had the bolts ground off and stood roped open. As the officer stamped her feet and paced along the road to keep warm, so Jessica crossed the road, hiding behind a parked van. The officer repeated the circuit and Jessica slipped into the park, unseen. Standing in the shadows, she watched the officer complete another lap. She stamped through Jessica's footprints, left clearly in the snow. Once past the gate, Jessica continued through the park. The exit gate was similarly damaged and roped open. A single police officer sat in a panda car, the engine running for the heat. Jessica slipped out of the park and headed along the A-Road towards Somerstown.

Not knowing the back streets in this area, Jessica walked along the trunk road, which later joined the main London Road out of town. She pulled the hood around her ears and strode as confidently as possible, despite the worsening pain in her foot. A single gritting lorry passed. Not seeing Jessica, the operator showered her with grit. Several police cars passed with blues flashing and sometimes sirens blasting.

Over an hour after crashing from the motorbike, Jessica turned left onto Wellington Street. She picked her way amongst the concrete towers and red brick social housing of Somerstown. Only a stone's throw from the main A2030 city thoroughfare, and the main commercial district beyond, Jessica found herself on deserted streets again.

'Got any fags?'

Jessica let out a yelp as a youth skidded to a halt in her path, his BMX showering her feet with snow.

'Christ! You could have given me a heart attack. And no, I don't smoke. Neither should you at your age.'

'Fuck you!'

Jessica barely made out the features of the youth under his hoodie and scarf. She guessed he had yet to reach his teens. Two other boys appeared on BMX bikes and circled Jessica.

'Give us some money, then.'

'I haven't got any. Now go home.'

'Your phone then.'

'Fuck you!' mimicked Jessica.

'I've got a knife!'

'So have I.' Jessica lied.

'Let us see your tits, then.'

Jessica shook her head and pushed past the youth, his worn trainers slipping in the snow.

'I only show my tits to men, not children.'

The other youths laughed, catching up with Jessica.

'You lost?'

'No.'

'Where are you going?'

'Mind your own business.'

'Why are there police everywhere?'

'How should I know? Ask them.'

'If you aren't lost, why are you going down a block end? Nothing but flats and lockups down there. Are you looking for River's Street?'

'Maybe.'

'That is back the way you came. Why is your chin bleeding?'

'I slipped in the snow. Look! Look, ok. I am lost. I am looking for Devil's Asshole. Do you know it?'

'Maybe.'

'Please take me there.'

'If you show me your tits, I will.'

'If you mention my tits again, I will get my boyfriend to break your legs with an iron bar. He knows who you are.'

The youths stared at Jessica and then at each other.

'What do we get for showing you Devil's Asshole, then?'

'You get to keep your legs unbroken.'

'Why don't you get your big boyfriend to show you?'

'He is with his wife tonight. Don't mention me to anyone. If he or his wife finds out - you've guessed it, broken legs.'

The first boy to have spoken shrugged, spun around on his bike, and sped off in the direction he came from, followed immediately by the second boy. Jessica and the third boy watched the pair disappear into the gloom and spray of slush. Jessica returned her gaze to the third youth.

'Ok, I will show you. We aren't really welcome in the precinct – that is *Parade Possie's* turf. But I'm not scared of them. They are just kids.' He pushed his scarf against his nose and blew snot. 'This way.'

Jessica knew the police would look for three women escapees, assuming they had not yet caught one, or both, of the others. She felt slightly less conspicuous walking with the youth. He chatted as they walked; Jessica grunted an occasional yes or no. She wanted to

141

formulate a plan, but there were so many variables and factors beyond her control. She could not trust DC Dolly, but he was her only hope of avoiding a long custodial sentence, even if they reduced the charges to assault. Jessica contemplated going public with Special Branch's, probably illegal, bribe and blackmail. However, she realised she was the David to their Goliath, except she was the accused, the baddy, and did not have a rock, let alone a sling.

To stand any chance of keeping DC Dolly onside, she needed to stay close to Shamima until he brought Jessica back in from the cold. She also needed to contact Mrs Wilson and keep her informed of his promises and her own decisions – however misinformed they may be.

'Is Dolly your girlfriend?'

'Dolly?'

'You just said you needed to talk with Dolly.'

'Did I? No, Dolly is my dog. Is it much further?'

The youth stopped in the shadows of a vandalised and boarded-up public toilet.

'I shouldn't really be here. This is Bedford Street, way out of my patch. Cross here and follow St James's Street, like for less than one minute. On your right is Somerstown Parade. Walk between the shops. Past the post office is a tiny alleyway, which goes to the service road between Somerstown Parade and Somerstown East Precinct. It runs behind and between the shops. Good luck. See you later.'

'Wait! Where is Devil's Asshole?'

'The service road is Devil's Asshole. I hope your boyfriend is waiting for you. It is not the nicest part of Somerstown.'

'Is there a nice part?'

The boy stared Jessica in the eye for a few seconds. Then down at her chest.

'I don't suppose …'

'No! Now fuck off. Go home and get warm. Oh, and thanks.'

Chapter Ten

Jessica steeled herself. She felt bitterly cold and the icy wind bit at her exposed flesh. Her injured foot was agony and her nose, fingers, and feet ached with the cold. She took a deep breath, crossed Bedford Street, and walked down the centre of St James's Road. Snow piled and drifted across the pavement. The snowploughed, and gritted, main Somerstown concourse was free of all traffic. The police vehicles criss-crossing the city did not venture into the inner-city estates. Instead, they concentrated on the three road bridges and ferry ports off the island of Portsea. She turned right into the pedestrian concrete shopping precinct. Immediately ahead stood two police officers. Too late to avoid them, she continued straight ahead, head bowed against the icy wind and hood pulled around her face.

'No gloves, love?'

'I lost them.'

'You need to get home, love, or are you with this lot?'

The officer gestured towards an old ice-cream van parked in the pedestrian area. A loose group of young people stood around the van, stamping their feet against the cold.

'Yeah, with them.'

'Do you serve the soup, or are you a customer?'

'Does that matter to you, officer?'

The officer laughed.

'Just checking your welfare, love.'

'I am not your love, officer. And I am fine, thank you.'

The three stood in silence. Jessica needed to move away as soon as possible but did not want to appear skittish.

'Of course, Miss. I haven't seen you around here before.'

'That's what you said last time we spoke.'

'How did you cut your face?'

'I slipped in the snow. I need to get off now. Thanks for checking on me.'

'Ask them for a coat.'

'I will.'

'And gloves.'

'Good night.'

Jessica walked towards the ice-cream van, trying not to limp.

'Hi.'

'Hey. I don't suppose you have a warm drink, please? And some wipes and a sticking-plaster?'

'Sure. Step into the slightly less freezing van.'

The young woman pulled Jessica into the driving seat of the van. Warm air streamed from the heater and added to the warmth of the gas ring. Jessica sipped chicken soup from a paper cup.

'Oh dear. That looks sore. Shall I get you an Uber to A and E? I think it will need a stitch. We can pay for the Uber.'

'No. Just a plaster, please.'

'We are not permitted to administer first aid.'

As the woman spoke, she dabbed Jessica's split chin with a medicated wipe. Jessica's face was numb with the cold, and it took a moment to flinch at the sting of alcohol. The woman firmly pressed adhesive butterfly stitches across the split, pulling the wound closed. Finally, she applied a gauze and a large plaster to hold it all together.

'So, if anyone asks, you did all that yourself.'

'Thanks.'

'You are limping.'

'I twisted my ankle when I slipped. It is only a sprain.'

'Lucky we are still here. We are doing a double shift tonight. We want to make sure we see everyone here at least once. Hopefully, we will get a couple of hot drinks in people's bellies. Where are you sleeping?'

'Here.'

'In Devil's Asshole?'

'Yeah.'

'I hope you have more than a hoodie and jumper.'

'I haven't, to be honest.'

'I am not judging. I am just thinking aloud. That is a nice jumper, and you obviously aren't using anything. Isn't there somewhere you can stay? Are you running from someone?'

'Something like that.'

'I can call a refuge for you.'

'No, thanks.'

'Or get you in a shelter. The council has opened an emergency weather shelter in Fratton. I can get you an Uber to there.'

'I just need an old coat and blanket. I will sort something for myself in the morning.'

'If you survive the night.'

Jessica shrugged. The woman continued.

'We don't have coats in the van, but we have *salvation coffins*.'

'Sorry?'

'Waxed cardboard boxes full of goodies. Inside is a sleeping bag, gloves, scarf, puffer-jacket, and thick socks. There is also cake, juice, and a bible. You can sleep inside the box. In this weather, it might last a couple of nights, but you are still dangerously exposed to the cold.'

'A bible?'

'The boxes are from the Salvation Army.'

Jessica sniggered and then laughed. The woman nervously joined in until she saw the tears punctuating Jessica's laughter. She hugged Jessica close.

The group gave Jessica the box, slung over her shoulder with the plastic strap fitted. She also took a paper cup of vegetable soup with a lid fitted and a warm hotdog in an icy cold bun. She ate and drank as she walked to the post office and into the underbelly of Portsmouth.

Some shops shone security lamps fitted high on the rear walls to illuminate small sections of the alley. Jessica made out prostrate figures wrapped in sleeping bags and scraps of polythene sheet against the cold. Some had piles of belongings around them in doorways. Others had no obvious possessions, squeezing themselves into the near non-existent strip of protection offered by the overhanging roof eaves.

Jessica saw a young man sat in his sleeping bag, next to a *Salvation Coffin*. He leant against one end of a shuttered double entrance.

'Sorry, may I sleep here, just for one night?'

'Sure, if you really want to. Is that a hint of a Norfolk accent?'

'No.' Jessica lied; not sure how much information they had published about the escapees. She had lived briefly in Devon and Bristol; she now affected a west country accent. 'Devon. Many moons ago.'

'Why are you here?'

'Why are you here?'

The young man laughed, exposing rotten and missing teeth.

'Work.'

'What sort of work?'

'You really are out of your depth. Get to a shelter. You shouldn't be here.'

'Why don't you get to a shelter?'

'Oh, for fuck's sake! Shut up making a noise!' screamed the adjacent salvation coffin. With the box shaking from side to side, the figure of a painfully thin girl appeared, dragging a sleeping bag behind. She collapsed the box, sitting on the cardboard in her sleeping-bag.

'Sorry. I didn't realise you were sleeping.'

The young man spoke, nodding towards the girl. 'That is why. She is rude, breaks every rule, and fights the staff. We might try the emergency shelter; they don't know us there. We might even get an entire night in before she kicks off and gets us chucked out.' He shrugged.

The girl watched Jessica wipe the remains of her bread bun around the empty inside of the cup.

'What work are you looking for? I could put in a word.'

'What work is available?'

'You know. Most things.'

'Like what?'

'Maybe running or selling dope. But the gangs don't know you, so maybe not. Porn, shop lifting. Do you hustle?'

'No. I …'

'You should hustle. Guys will pay top money for you.'

'No. Thanks. I will sort something in the morning. I'm looking for my, you know, boyfriend.'

'Are you with the Polish?'

Jessica remembered the motorbike rider's accent. 'Yeah. But I got a bit lost.'

'We saw them earlier. They might be back later.'

'The Polish guys? With motorbikes?'

'No motorbikes. But there were two men and two girls. They probably went into the nail bar.'

'Yeah, that will be them. One of the guys is my boyfriend. Where is the nail bar?'

'Eastern Parade. That, there, is the delivery back entrance.' The woman pointed to a rusty, painted double door of an indeterminate colour under the dim yellow lighting.

Jessica approached the door, stepping over a full sleeping-bag wrapped in a polythene sheet. She rattled the door by the bolt against the hinges. After a few attempts, she gave up and returned to her place with the couple.

'How do I get to the front of the shop, please?'

'Retrace your steps. Take the first alley on the left and left again in front of the shops. But …' The woman glanced at her companion. He continued.

'There is filth everywhere. Something has kicked off at the prison – we heard there was a riot or something. Your boyfriend might not appreciate you bringing any attention to the front of the shop, at this time of night.'

Jessica collapsed her box and sat on the flattened cardboard against the cold ground. She unzipped the sleeping bag and draped it over herself, her knees pulled to her chest and her head bowed. She listened to the couple talking about trying to pull some money together before slipping into a fitful sleep.

'Hey. Wakey, wakey. Guess who's here?'

Jessica woke, cold and confused. Every inch of her body ached from the two traffic incidents and the cold. She pulled the sleeping bag from over her head and blinked at two figures stood by the steel door, now opened a few inches. One figure kicked the sleeping bag laid outside the metal door. The occupant reluctantly rolled and crawled away, allowing the door to open further. Jessica sprung to her knees and as she stood, her female neighbour grabbed her arm.

'You not going to thank me for our hospitality?'

'Thanks. I appreciate it.'

Jessica saw the young woman's face in the light spilling from the opened door. Her skin was pale and translucent, her nostrils sore and angry, her lips lined with sores.

'Have you anything to sell, or any change?'

'No, sorry. Look, I really haven't. Sorry. You can have my sleeping-bag and everything. Look, I am really sorry.'

Jessica pulled her arm free and walked to the two figures. Inside the room were three young oriental men, heads bowed and eyes wide with fear. They wore black jeans, white trainers, and black puffer jackets, inadequate against the winter cold.

'You love, need to clear off, before I clear you off.'

The taller of the original two men spoke. He was calm and intimidating, sounding like an experienced nightclub bouncer, his accent thick Polish.

A third European appeared from inside the shop. Pushing the three Orientals ahead of him, they left with the remaining European and disappeared into the dark alley. Before the Polish bouncer could speak again, Jessica interrupted.

'I am supposed to be here, dumbass! Your mate crashed and almost killed me.'

The bouncer looked up and down the alley. He stared at the couple in the opposite doorway, until they looked away, and pulled Jessica into the shop, pulling closed the doors.

'You idiot. Why did you come here?'

'Because this is where I am supposed to be, idiot.'

The room was constructed like a concrete garage. Two walls were painted scarlet red, with a massive round bed pushed into the corner. Two video cameras sat high on tripods with camera-lights and microphones; the lights switched off. A fat, balding man sat in a comfy chair to one side of the *film-set*, playing with a *stills* camera. Two young women slept on the bed, huddled together under a grey duvet without a cover. Jessica saw the face of one girl, probably no older than mid-teens.

The bouncer pushed Jessica towards a second door and the front room of the shuttered shop. Low green emergency lights illuminated the way to a second door and a set of steep stairs leading to the first floor.

Bouncer leant past Jessica, opening a door into the room. A blast of hot air and light washed over Jessica as he pushed her into the room.

Two women stood from a sofa opposite the door.

'Jessica!' the two women shouted in unison.

'Shamima. Alisha. Good to see you safe.'

Alisha took a step forward, arms extended for a hug. Shamima pulled her back roughly.

'What are you doing here, Jessica? Where is Bashira? I told you to stay in the van!'

'I know Shamima. That is what I said. But Bashira ordered me out, and then she passed out. I think she has a concussion.'

Shamima threw up her hands.

'Great! Just great! How did you get here?'

'I hitched a motorbike lift half the way and walked the rest. I …'

'If you have been seen, you are in deep trouble! What's up with you? Who have you spoken with or seen?'

'No one Shamima, honestly.' Jessica remembered the homeless man in the hospital grounds, the boys on bikes, the group working the soup kitchen and the couple huddled in a doorway opposite. Worst of all, she remembered the two police officers. If the police were suspicious, she hoped their concerns got back to DC Dolly. 'No one. The motorbike rider was a bit of a mess. He drove into a gravestone. He gave me directions to get here.'

'Great. Go upstairs and wait.'

'Wait for what? How are we getting off the island? It takes the filth two minutes to lockdown Pompey – there are only three road bridges and the train bridge.'

'It's ok Jess. We are …'

'Shut up Alisha! You do as you are told, Jess. Go upstairs and wait. You are risking everything, and I am in no mood to explain myself to you. Move it!'

Bouncer yanked Jessica backwards by the hair and pushed her into the stairwell. The second flight of stairs was steeper and rickety. The door at the top led into an attic room with a slanting roof of bare concrete tiles.

'Oh, we have another guest. We were expecting you.' A man in his late thirties stood and looked Jessica up and down. He had ginger hair and a beard full of crisps and detritus.

Bouncer spoke. 'I am not sure this is who we are expecting. She is not to leave this room.'

'Take a seat.'

'I am ok, for a minute.'

'Well, at least stand under the heater. Hungry?'

'Always.' Jessica stood under the stream of tepid air from a fan heater screwed to a roof joist. As the man moved to a camping-gaz stove sat on a table, Jessica sat on a beanbag under the heat.

'Tomato soup or baked beans?'

'Either please.'

Although the room felt icy-cold and draughty, Jessica closed her eyes against the stream of warmer air. She was about to drift asleep sitting up, when the man woke her by thrusting a cold dessert bowl into her chest. The contents were a mixture of a cheap tin of tomato soup with a cheaper tin of beans floating on the surface.

'Best eat before they get cold.'

The meal was barely warm and cooling rapidly against the cold bowl. Jessica spooned the contents into her mouth, swallowing while barely chewing.

'Nice?'

'No, shit. But thanks anyway. How are we getting away from Portsmouth?'

'You don't know?' Jessica shrugged at the man. 'I am not the one to tell you. You are … You were staying with the other two? You are one of them?'

'Yes of course. I am not the pizza delivery girl. We escaped together. Shamima is a bit grumpy. Her mate didn't make it.'

'Dead? Fuck!'

'No, not dead. She bumped her head. Just tell me what happens to me, us three, next.'

The door opened, Shamima, Alisha, and Bouncer walked in. Bouncer carried a large, seemingly empty, suitcase. Shamima spoke.

'You listen to me very carefully Jess. If you disobey me again, you are on your own.'

'I didn't actually …'

'Listen very carefully. You don't want me to cut you loose. You already know too much.'

Shamima flicked her head towards Bouncer. Jessica understood the implied threat and nodded, wishing now she had handed herself in to the two police officers or stayed put in the prison van. She swallowed hard. Shamima continued.

'You are going first. You talk to nobody on your journey, nor when you get to London. Understood?' Jessica nodded. 'We are following behind. We are going a different route. You are costing my organisation a lot of money. This lot doesn't come cheap.' She gestured again to the Polish bouncer. 'It will be cheaper if I sell you on now. Understood? But we are sisters. Are you still up for helping the cause – in a way that *I* see fit?'

'Yes, of course. Anything to stay out of nick.'

'Jess! You need to start by keeping your fat gob shut!'

'Sorry. I thought …' Jessica blushed at being chastised in front of the others. Then blushed deeper for having let such an insignificant act affect her, in the middle of this mess.

'You are forcing us onto our back foot with your recklessness, Jess. Have you ever been told how reckless you act?'

'I have, sorry. My husband …'

'So, we must move fast. You are going by road. Get in the case.'

'No! Seriously, Shamima, I can't. I'm claustrophobic. I can't. I don't mean I don't want to; I mean, I physically can't.'

'No problem. Stay here with our Polish friends.'

Alisha stepped forward, brushing away Shamima's grip.

'Jess, please do as Shamima says. These animals will film what they do to you, and then you might not survive, or they will keep you imprisoned. Please.'

Jessica began crying, backing away from the case. Alisha spoke again.

'Sham, please. Make her. She can't stay with this lot.' She gestured towards Bouncer, unable to look at him.

'This is turning into a committee. I am running out of patience. Bouncer, get her in the case now, dead or alive.'

Pulling a rubber truncheon from the back of his belt, Bouncer took a step towards Jessica. She automatically took a defensive kickboxing stance through her tears, facing down her assailant. The first blow caught the top of her thigh. As she twisted away in pain, the second blow hit her buttocks and the third her kidneys. Screaming in pain, Bouncer picked her off the floor, face down, by the hair and one hand grabbing her groin from behind and between her legs. She felt hair ripping from her scalp. A moment later she was in the case, Bouncer folding in her body and limbs as he zipped it closed.

'And shut her up!'

'Really?' replied Bouncer. 'I was going to put her on the coach screaming and kicking like a bear having bile harvested.'

The zip opened a few inches. Jessica thrust her hand into the gap to force the zip open further. She felt the needle enter her wrist. Almost immediately she calmed, feeling the pressure of the injection inflate her vein. She felt vomit run warm over her chin and a welcomed peace wash over her. All the pain left her body. All worries left her mind. She let her bladder go. Background voices were clear, but of no importance.

'I am adding that to your bill. Heroin doesn't come cheap anymore. Cost of living crisis and all that.'

Jessica smiled at Bouncer's joke. The case tilted and banged down the stairs as Jessica nodded asleep.

Chapter Eleven

Jessica spent the first part of her journey nodding asleep. She tried unsuccessfully to remember the many good times in her life. Good times were comparative and offset by bad times. In the heroin haze, Jessica felt neither good nor bad. She *experienced* the cold, the stench of her own vomit in the confined space, the cold wet patch between her legs. Her skin prickled like the worst sunburn in a cold bath – but none of it mattered.

She felt herself loaded into the hold of a coach and heard the airbrake release. The journey was slow and deliberate in the snow. On one occasion, the coach stopped and the hold door opened. There were voices and torchlight penetrated the zip of her prison and around the stitched seams. But Jessica did not care.

The coach stopped again sometime later. Her suitcase was pulled from the hold and bumped onto the ground. A moment later, she was lifted into a different vehicle. The warmth from the interior eventually penetrated the suitcase. Jessica felt warmer, she no longer disliked being cold, nor enjoyed being warm. The case bumped up a set of stairs and a door slammed.

The case opened. Jessica spilled out onto the carpeted floor.

'Are you ok sister?'

'Yeah. I think so.'

'Can you move?'

'No.'

Jessica tried to open her eyes, but the light blinded her. She lacked the motivation to push through the discomfort.

'We are going to undress you.'

'Ok.'

Jessica felt the hands on her. They were female and lacked the strength and brute force of Bouncer. With her leggings, jogging bottoms, and pants removed, the warm air rushed to her wet thighs. As they pulled off her jumper and top, they caught her in a way that would normally send her into a claustrophobic panic. She smiled to herself as one female held her under the arms, and another tugged the clothes free.

Her head lolling from side to side, they half carried, and half dragged, her across the floor. She experienced a not unpleasant sensation of burning, as her bottom scraped across the carpet. Jessica felt the cold water from the shower blast over her naked body, followed by a scalding hot, and eventually a pleasant warmth.

'Sorry, sorry. Are you ok, sister?'

'I'm fine.'

'May I wash you?'

'Whatever.'

Jessica awoke in bed. The sheets were clean. A thin blanket covered her in the warm room. A bedside lamp glowed. She sat up. An Asian man and woman sat on another bed, playing with their phones.

'Hey.'

They both looked up.

'Are you ok?'

'Sure. Is Shamima here?'

The couple looked at each other and back to Jessica.

'Hungry?'

'I've been hungry since Christmas morning. Now I'm starving.'

Jessica sneezed. Her joints ached and her stomach cramped. She spoke again.

'Excuse me. I must have a cold.' She had a fit of sneezing, which continued as she shook, and her stomach churned. 'Fuck. Sorry.'

'Take your time. There's water there and paracetamol. Can I help?'

Jessica shook her head. Still sneezing, she reached for the water and tablets.

'We have some dahl. Or would you rather …'

'Dahl, please. Yes. Is it home cooked?'

The woman opposite laughed.

'Of course, it is. Dahl is always home cooked. Isn't it?' She looked at her companion, who shrugged a response. 'In bed? Or are you ready to get up?'

Jessica sat at the Formica table wearing a baggy, loaned T-shirt. Her clothes confiscated; the couple promised a new set as soon as the shops opened. While Jessica ate her third bowl of dahl with flat bread, the man washed and dressed her chin. Pulling her injured leg forward, he bathed her foot in salty water, dried, and applied antiseptic cream. Jessica's T-shirt fell from one shoulder. The man rubbed his thumb over the syringe wound DC Dolly had inflicted.

'What's this?' His thumb found a lump under her flesh. He rubbed it between his thumb and forefinger. 'Does it hurt? There is something there.'

'I fell onto a chair leg.'

'Something embedded in the wound. You need to get that sorted before it goes mank.'

Jessica nodded.

'Where's the other girl? The girl who helped wash me. Where are Shamima and Alisha, please? Who are you? Where am I?'

The couple exchanged glances. The woman spoke.

'You told me your name, Jess. I wish you hadn't. Please ask no more questions. You keep reeling off names. I wish you to stop, please.'

'Can I go outside? Am I a prisoner?'

'We do not hold you prisoner, Jess. We were told to expect you. They said you wanted to come here. Obviously, you can't go out into the cold wearing just a T-shirt. You can't go out wearing your … You can't wear clothes that might be recognised. There are people looking for you.

'Look Jess. You have been through a lot. You are now with friends. Just chill, eat as much as you can. Sleep as much as you can. Regain your strength –

mental and physical. Just wait until … someone comes to speak with you.'

'When will Shamima and …'

'All I can say is someone will contact you in a day or two. What's the hurry? We have music and a television. I am afraid you can't have any news stations, but we can watch films and shows together.'

Jessica released a long sigh.

Shamima and Alisha arrived late the following day. They were exhausted and hungry, following a similar routine on arrival as Jessica had – showering, eating, sleeping, and eating again. There were two single and two double beds in Jessica's room. Shamima and Alisha took the double beds.

The four women stayed in the rooms as the man shopped, with a list of clothes and groceries. Returning two hours later, he piled the goods on the fourth bed, said his goodbyes and left the women alone.

Jessica made Turkish menemen for her roommates to eat with crusty tiger bread. Sat around the table, Jessica started the conversation. She needed to move the situation along, gain some credible information and share part of it with DC Dolly. She decided the time had come to involve Mrs Wilson in her plot. Jessica was especially worried of being captured and arrested before having enough information to make her a viable commodity. Until arrest, she would also keep her powder dry with Shamima – in case fleeing abroad was the better option to stay out of prison.

'You were both fitter than me after your journey.'

Alisha squeezed Jessica's wrist from across the table.

'It was awful seeing you treated so badly by the Polish. But it would have been worse if you'd stayed. How was your trip?'

'The chemical one, or the journey? For the first time since returning from India, I just didn't care about anything. The relief was amazing, a kind of peace. But I will never take heroin again. It's so powerful; absolute power. And absolute power corrupts absolutely.

'Talking of which Shamima, we need to talk.'

Shamima looked up from her plate to stare at Jessica, a fork halfway to her open mouth. The other two women looked down at their food as Jessica held the stare.

'Ok Jess. I am very unhappy you are here. I nearly had the Polish return what was left of you to the police. But you are here now. You will need to work your passage, understood?'

'Sure. Anything for the cause.'

'Don't you *'the cause'* me Jess. You are like a barnacle; just hanging on for the ride out of here.'

'I am not sure that analogy works. You would have scraped off a barnacle, but here I am.'

'And like I say, you will need to work your passage.'

'In return, you can get me to Turkey?'

'In return, I will let you live.'

The other two stopped chewing. Alisha swallowed hard, the spicy egg making her cough.

'Do you know something, Shamima? You don't scare me,' Jessica lied. 'I can't live in prison. If I can earn my way to freedom, then fine. If not, then whatever. But you need to talk to me. We can't just sit around here waiting for the police to find us. Say what you need and get me to Turkey.'

'Ok. We want you and Alisha to deliver something to the naval base in Portsmouth.'

'Can't you send it by post?'

'Wait Shamima! I can do it alone. We agreed.'

'*Agreed* Alisha? I am not aware that I asked for your agreement. It is my decision. That burden is mine. You will take the glory, just the same.'

'It's not about my taking …'

Shamima placed a silencing finger on Alisha's lips and turned her attention back to Jessica.

'Thanks for the postal advice, Jess. I want to save the stamp and send you two instead.'

'What's in the parcel?'

'Do you care?'

'Um, yes. Actually, I do.'

'Shamima …'

'Quiet Alisha. Money Jess. I want a bag of money delivered to my contact in the base.'

'It would be easier to give them the money outside the base.'

'Goodness, I am having no end of advice today. I am sure Alisha can cope alone and you may have just become suddenly surplus.'

'I am not saying I won't help, just trying to understand.'

'Don't try. We all have our parts to play. Mine is to understand.'

'Surely Portsmouth is the last place to send Alisha? Or me, even.'

'The police will be diverted in their efforts, on the day. We will dress you in a pretty western frock, making you less conspicuous as a mixed couple, rather than send Alisha alone.'

'And I get Alisha and the box into the dockyard? The Historic Dockyard area? Why don't I just go alone?'

'And keep the money?'

'Charming.'

'But you can get Alisha and the package into the Historic Dockyard without being searched? And to The Mary Rose museum?'

'Easy.'

'Easy? Perhaps I don't need you after all.'

'Easy for me, I meant.'

'What day is it? Time flies when you are having fun.' The fourth roommate responded.

'Today is Thursday 5th, Shamima.'

'Ok Fatima. Can you pick up a nice dress for Jessica, please? Tomorrow. Do you need to take Mehmet or your sister?'

'Can I go with her, please? I need to get some air; you know how claustrophobic I feel.'

'Good idea Jess. Let's all go. We could have a girl's day out. See how many CCTV cameras we can get ourselves on!'

'Not as many cameras as on a journey from London to inside a secure military base in the middle of Portsmouth, home to the British Navy, that's for sure. Just a walk to the shops and back. I'll keep my hat pulled low, scarf up, false moustache and glasses. Please Shamima. I could go with Alisha.'

'Ok. Go with Fatima. But make sure you cover up. All the time. Understood? And I like the glasses and moustache idea. Fatima, can you arrange that please?'

'Not a problem, Shamima. We will be fine without Mehmet.'

Jessica and Alisha sat in front of the television, neither watching the film. Alisha rested her head on Jessica's lap, sleeping in snatches following her journey of the previous evening. Jessica idly ran her fingers through Alisha's hair, planning how she might send a message to Mrs Wilson and DC Dolly. She had written both their mobile numbers on the back of her hand when in prison. Thankfully Fatima had noted the numbers for Jessica, before scrubbing them off, in the shower.

'Was it awful Jess? The heroin and being in the case? I cried all night thinking about you.'

'I can barely remember it now. Is that how you travelled?'

'No. The Polish took us to the Isle of Wight, hidden in an empty fuel tank of a day-fisher boat. We then climbed into a private plane to Elstree. A harbour police launch searched the boat, but they didn't find us. The tank smelt of diesel, and I was seasick, but not as bad as your experience. The plane is a regular service taking private mail and hospital supplies between London and the Isle of Wight. Apparently, there was a search by the police looking for us. We got in after the search by hiding on the airfield and then clambering in as the plane taxied over to take off. Quite exciting, actually. This end was easy. They know how to avoid all CCTV between here and the tube station.'

'Are you ok doing the drop?'

'No Jess, I am petrified. I think that is why Shamima wants you to go as well; to give me some support. I am so scared.'

'It isn't money. Is it Alisha?'

'Why do you think not?'

'They wouldn't take the risk for money. They would simply transfer it offshore or something.'

'Shamima said they stole it in a bank van robbery, which is why it is in cash.'

'I am not convinced, Alisha. Why risk smuggling it into the naval base? The recipient will only have to smuggle it out again.'

Alisha shrugged her shoulders against Jessica's legs.

'I am just doing as I am asked, Jess. Perhaps it is leaving the base by naval ship, I don't know.'

'What if it is something … terrible?'

'Please don't Jess. We are at war with the west. Shamima has asked me to do one small job. The Imam said it would see me enter heaven when my time comes.'

'Shit! That doesn't make me feel any happier.'

'Please Jess. Support me or just keep quiet. It is not too late to say you can't go with me.'

'Shamima seems sold on the idea. What do you think about her threats?'

'I love Shamima. She is pious and strong. But I know she has killed. I think you need to treat her carefully, Jess.'

'I was only joking about the glasses and moustache! Have you got a cigar, as well?'

Fatima and Alisha laughed along with Jessica. Shamima spoke.

'It is only for between here and the tube station. It suits you; you look dramatic.'

The women continued to laugh. With her hat pulled down, her scarf pulled up, and huge, thick, opaque glasses, there was little flesh showing. She took the folding white cane from Fatima.

'There Jess, look at yourself in the mirror. You really look blind.'

This time Shamima joined in the laughing as Jessica pretended to check her reflection blindly. She purposely faced the wall away from the mirror.

'Yes, I look gorgeously desperate.'

Fatima helped Jessica into her thick black coat and fastened the buttons, handing her gloves.

'Stay close to me…'

'Obviously! I won't be riding a Boris Bike, that's for sure.'

'Once we get on the tube, put the stick away. Once any passengers have got off or replaced, take the glasses off and you can see again!'

'Laudy Laudy it's a miracle! The blind are cured!'

'And we do the opposite coming back. That way, if something goes wrong, you can't say where we are.'

'You really don't trust me, do you?'

'It is safer this way.' Shamima responded to the question.

'Oh my Lord, I'm hearing voices!'

The women laughed again.

'Ease off the blaspheming, Jess. It is the only sin our Lord will not forgive.' Shamima spoke with no humour. The giggling immediately stopped. 'Enjoy your taste of freedom.'

Holding Fatima's arm, Jessica allowed herself to be led through the door, down concrete steps and into the street. Jessica could see grubby cobbles out the bottom of her opaque glasses. They turned left onto a paving slabbed path. Slush clung to the shallow gutter close to shop fronts. There were people on the pavement.

She occasionally saw hurried feet passing close by, wearing boots or office heals.

'Here we are. Slowly down the steps.'

The tube train screamed into the station behind a rush of tepid air. The doors swished open. Few people made allowances for Jessica's apparent disability as they jostled her, stepping onto the carriage.

'Ok, sit here.'

Fatima eased Jessica back into a seat. She folded her white cane and slipped it into her bag. The train juddered to a halt, and the doors clattered open.

'Ok Jess, take the glasses off.'

Jessica looked around the third full carriage as the train pulled away from Shepherd's Bush station. She saw ordinary people leading ordinary lives. She took a deep breath and sighed. A man in his fifties sat diagonally opposite Jessica, two seats from Fatima. He saw her looking and winked. Jessica looked away. A younger woman sat next to the man. Jessica smelt cider on her breath from across the aisle. The young woman tried to read the man's newspaper over his shoulder. He moved away. The young woman offered an open cider can for Fatima to take a drink. Fatima rolled her eyes at Jessica and turned away from the woman. The woman sang along to the hiss of her iPhone AirPods, staring directly at Jessica. The song was a Dolly Parton release, *Nine to Five*.

'You like country music?'

'No, not really.'

Fatima shook her head at Jessica, silently discouraging her from speaking with the stranger. She stifled a smirk.

'Cider?' Jessica shook her head. 'You will like this one, by Dolly.' The woman joined in with the opening to *Jolene*. She moved over to sit next to Jessica, taking out one of her AirPods and tucking it under Jessica's hat and against her ear. The woman continued to sing *Jolene* as Jessica moved to push the AirPod and the woman away. She heard the man's voice from the AirPod.

'Can you hear me, Mrs Taylor? Nod for the young lady.'

Jessica recognised the voice of DC Dolly. She faced the woman and nodded. The woman nodded in time with the non-existent music.

'Are you alone?'

Jessica swayed her head from side to side. The woman tapped a message on her phone.

'Are you being watched now?'

Jessica nodded.

'The young woman has slid a phone behind your back. Will you be able to retrieve it and use it later?'

Jessica nodded.

'Is anything happening?'

Jessica nodded.

'Today?'

Jessica swayed her head.

'Tomorrow?'

Jessica shrugged and frowned at the woman, as if undecided about the song. She caught Fatima's eye as she giggled behind her hand. Jessica smiled back.

'Are you in danger?'

Jessica nodded.

'Imminent?'

Jessica shrugged, frowned, and finally swayed her head.

'Contact me as soon as you can. Stay close to Shamima. I implanted you with a tracker. We know where you are most of the time, depending on signals. Obviously not on the Tube, but we know where you are staying. Some good news, try not to punch the air: we raided and arrested a Polish people smuggling gang based in Portsmouth. We released two young women into Emergency Foster Care and are tracking down various Vietnamese slaves farming cannabis around the city. A tall, thickset trafficker was shot and injured as he attacked an armed officer with a rubber bar.'

Jessica smiled broadly towards Fatima and punched the air, as if celebrating the end of the song. Fatima laughed louder, clutching her sides.

'You are already making a difference. Hang in there.'

Jessica handed back the AirPod as the woman stood to pursue the man with the paper.

'Well, that is three minutes of my life I will never get back.'

Fatima laughed, shaking her head. 'Nobody, ever, talks to people on the Tube. You are so provincial, but so funny. No wonder Alisha has the hots for you!'

Jessica frowned at Fatima, shaking her head. 'A good Muslim girl like Alisha? I don't think so. Come on, let's buy me a frock and sexy boots.'

As the train slowed, Jessica stood, holding the phone behind her back, and then tucked it into the elasticated cuff of her coat.

'I need the loo before we head back.'

'I have to come with you, Jess, sorry.'

'Um, not that sort of *loo,* Fatima.'

'It doesn't matter. I will wait outside the cubical.'

'I can't go if I know people can hear. That *thing* of mine has got worse since prison.'

'Not an option, sorry.'

Having slipped the phone inside the waistband of her jeans, Jessica left her coat, and shopping, with Fatima by the basins, and entered the cubical alone. She sat on the toilet, straining to make as much noise as possible. She tapped a message on the phone with both thumbs.

"Jax. Me, Jess. I can't call. Someone is listening."

The reply was immediate.

"Jess!!! It don't work like that. How do I know is you??"

"Tough. Its me. I'm working with DC Dolly Williamson. He injected me with a tracker. He knows where I am."

"A tracker?? You need to hand yourself in – NOW!!"

"It was me who led them to the Pompey traffickers bust. I need you to know. I am in London near

Goldhawk Tube. I think out station, turn left, left onto cobbled alley/path/mews, first floor flat. No more than ten mins walk from station. Talk to Dolly – he needs to know you know."

"You need to get somewhere safe. HAND YOURSELF IN!!!'

Jessica flicked to contacts and started a message to the only entry.

"Dolly, you prick! I can't talk. Hammersmith with Alisha, Shamima, a kid called Fatima, I think her sister and a guy called Mehmet. Soon Alisha and me deliver a pack to Pompey dockyard. We will come through Gosport Alliance submarine museum. Then Dockyard by water taxi. Don't know what is in pack. They say money. I don't think so."

"When?"

"Not sure. Had to be ready today. Maybe tomorrow."

"Shit. Tomorrow is a big day in the dockyard."

"???"

"Can't say. Go with pack and Alisha for now. Cut loose Shamima."

"No fucking way!! Come and get me!!!"

"No. Do as instructed. This is big. You will be a hero."

"A dead one?"

"Who knows? Can you bin phone?"

"I'm on loo."

"Flush it, properly!!"

'Jess? You still alive?'

'Just finished Fatima. Don't rush me. I swear one day I will own a soundproofed, fortified bathroom!'

To avoid any suspicion by flushing the toilet twice, Jessica wiped herself and, rolling up her sleeve, pushed the phone through the detritus of the toilet bowl until she had pushed the phone past the bend of the waste pipe, gagging. She flushed the toilet allowing the water to wash over her hand and forearm, before shaking and drying her arm on her jumper.

'You ok?'

'Sure. I'm six bowls of dahl down, but I'm fine. Can we grab a coffee and maybe visit a bar, or even just a library?'

Fatima laughed. 'Come on Jess, let's get home and I'll make you some dahl.'

Fatima agreed to buying fish and chips from a Chinese chippy across the road from Goldhawk Tube Station. Jessica had slipped on the glasses and produced her white cane as Fatima instructed.

'The smell of the chips is making me salivate!'

The server laughed at the remark and handed Jessica a small punnet of chips to eat, as she wrapped up four chip suppers to take back to the flat. On arrival, the flat was empty.

'Oh well, more for us.'

'Where are they?'

'How should I know, Jess? I have been out with you all day!'

'I don't like this, Fatima.'

'Don't be silly. It is fine. You are safe here.'

'I want to be with the others. Find out where they are and take me there. Please Fatima, please.'

'Hey! That is enough. I am sure they will be back later. We can reheat their suppers. All is ok.'

Jessica nodded, sitting on the edge of the sofa with Fatima holding both her hands.

'You are a lovely woman, Jess. It has been lovely to meet you. I think you are all three very brave. I think you will go soon, with Alisha. Look after both of you. Promise?'

Jessica nodded again.

Jessica lay on her back in Alisha's bed, taking comfort from the smell of Alisha's hair on the pillow. Her mind raced through events since returning from India. For the first time since attacking her husband and his friend, Jessica allowed herself to recall the fear on Priti's face. She remembered the sickening sound as she demolished her husband's face. She felt desperately sad for the loss of Priti's baby, but still not strong enough to empathise with the sadness the young woman must be feeling. Tears streamed down her cheeks. She thought of the young girls rescued from the traffickers, and smiled as she imagined the pain Bouncer must have felt as a bullet ripped through his flesh, muscle, and bone. Her current situation was far from satisfactory, but she appreciated the improvement over prison life. Jessica felt alive, the heroin having taught her how it felt to be dead, without a care. She wondered what was next for her, death by police shooting, a life on the run, or a rehabilitated hero. She would not return to prison.

Chapter Twelve

The sound of Fatima's phone jolted Jessica awake. Fatima sprang from bed with the phone clamped to her ear and left the room. Jessica strained to hear half the phone conversation, but Fatima spoke only a *yes* and an *ok, understood.*

'What's going on?'

'Nothing Jess. What shall we have for breakfast?'

'I'm not hungry! Who was on the phone?'

'I'd love you to cook some more Turkish menemen …'

'Fatima!'

'Ok, calm down. We have plenty of time. Shamima wants me to take you to Waterloo Station.'

'That it?'

'Jess, please calm down. You will sit towards the middle of the second first class carriage. Alisha will join you at Woking.'

'Fucking Woking! What is going on?'

'She will have the money in a bag. Just sit together until Portsmouth Harbour Station.'

'Then what?'

'You know better than me, Jess. Sit down and tell me your plan. Run through it with me.'

'Shit! Ok. We can catch the Gosport Ferry from The Hard outside the station. We will walk to HMS Alliance.'

'Is it far?'

'No. Twenty minutes maybe. Or we could get an Uber.'

'No Ubers, Jess. Hail a cab on the street or walk.'

'Ok. We can walk. Have you got our tickets for the Alliance?'

'No.'

'Ok. I need some money, I have nothing. I will buy us day tickets to see the submarine and the Historic Dockyard. It includes the water taxi. I'll include The Mary Rose. Shall we look around the Alliance?'

'I think you, and especially Alisha, will be too nervous. Do you need to visit the sub?'

'No. We can sit outside. Wait for the next submarine tour to start. Then catch the water taxi to the Dockyard.'

'How do you get to the Mary Rose?'

'It's just a walk. No security.'

'There might be extra security today. Be prepared.'

'Why?'

'There just might.'

'Fatima!'

Fatima punched a text into her phone and waited for the response.

'Ok. King Charles is visiting The Mary Rose and then HMS Prince of Wales, moored in the naval base.'

'Fuck. Fuck fuck fuck!'

'It is not a problem. The visit is not public knowledge. There is a rolling security blanket around the King. More waiting and queuing. The press will announce the visit once the King has left Portsmouth.

You need to act normal and keep Alisha *together*. Understood?'

Jessica nodded. 'Fuck.'

Jessica ate the spoonful of dahl on a slice of toast. As she washed it down with black coffee, bile rose in her throat. She stood to rush to the bathroom, but immediately vomited onto the kitchen table.

'Sorry. I'll clear it up.'

'No, you won't, Jess. Brush your teeth and let's get you dressed. I am afraid we need to play the blind game again. Ok? Last time.'

The Portsmouth Harbour train left Waterloo on time. Jessica clutched a bottle of SunnyD to stop her hands from shaking. At Woking, Alisha boarded the train with Shamima and Mehmet. She caught a brief glimpse of Mehmet's face as the three sat together a few seats away. His eyes were wide, his complexion jaundice in the carriage lights. He immediately looked away from Jessica. Shamima kept a tight grip around Alisha's shoulders.

Jessica looked around the carriage, hoping to see some backup from DC Dolly. Two burly men joined the train at Guildford. They wore rugby shirts under opened jackets and carried sports bags, but at Godalming they left the carriage.

The first-class carriage emptied further as the train moved through the stockbroker belt surrounding London. Jessica's companions were the only brown faces in the carriage once a black man, in a sharp suit and expensive trench coat, left at Haslemere. The two women wore hijabs. Jessica now saw the sense of having her travel with Alisha to help avoid unnecessary scrutiny from fellow travellers of the jittery Alisha. At Petersfield, Mehmet left the train without glancing in Jessica's direction. As the train pulled into Havant, Shamima hugged and kissed Alisha, before walking towards the rear carriage door. She stopped next to Jessica and knelt to adjust the zip on her boot.

'See you in Istanbul.'

Jessica rung the bottle of orange so hard that her thumb penetrated the thin plastic and sent a fountain of juice spilling over herself and onto the seats. Discarding the bottle onto the floor, she stood to walk forward to Alisha – Shamima keeping pace outside the window as she walked along the platform.

'Alisha. Are you ok?'

Jessica repeated the question and Alisha raised her face, nodding. Alisha clasped a book, wrapped in cloth with a black and gold design, against her chest.

'Hey Alisha. It is going to be a long journey if we don't speak.'

Alisha mumbled and rocked. When her response came, it was a whisper.

'I am ok Jess. You can get off at the next stop. I am ok.'

'I don't think so. Is that the money?'

Alisha nodded.

Jessica found her hand, still clasping the book, and forced her fingers to entwine with Alisha's.

'Alisha, it is just you and me now. They have all gone. Shamima is no more in our lives. Do you understand? It is just you and me.'

Alisha brought the book, with Jessica's hand, to touch her forehead and then her chest, looking upwards.

'Let me take the money, Alisha. Give me the bag.'

Alisha shook her head. 'I can't. It is fixed. They strapped it into my jacket.'

'So how do we deliver the bag if you can't take it off?'

Alisha began rocking and praying again.

'Alisha, honey. Talk to me. Shamima wants me to know everything. She just told me as she left the train. Shamima said *Jessica, tell Alisha to explain everything to you.* She said it is now my job to understand everything.'

Alisha nodded.

'Shamima said you will take me to The Mary Rose. I can't remember the directions. I think it is on a boat or a submarine. Jess, I am scared.'

'It's ok darling. This is why I am here. I will take you to The Mary Rose. What do we do once we are there?'

Alisha pulled a plastic electrical switch from the rucksack side pouch. The switch connected to the rucksack by an electrical cable. Taped around the switch was a mobile phone. As Alisha showed Jessica the switch, Jessica saw another thin wire wrapped and tied around Alisha's wrist. It snaked up the arm of her jacket. A similar wire, Jessica assumed the same one, then led from inside Alisha's jacket and connected to the switch.

'Fuck! Careful Alisha. Put it back, carefully.'

Alisha nodded, slipping the switch back into the rucksack.

'I must get this exactly right, Jess. I am going to tell you, then you can make sure I do it correctly. I thought Shamima said not to tell you. I am so confused. Jess, I think I have peed myself.'

'That doesn't matter, love. We can sort that in a minute. Shamima definitely wants you to tell me everything. She just said to me *Alisha has a bomb. She will explain everything.* Honestly, darling. She is worried you are scared and will get mixed up. She wants me to help you. You can ask her if you like.'

'She told you about the bomb?'

'Absolutely, she did. What do you have to remember?'

'At The Mary Rose, we join the queue or go into the café. This is very important, Jess. First, I push the button. That will release the buckle of the strap from around my back and through my coat. I then have exactly one minute to warn everyone and run away. Nobody needs to die, but it will send a message to the west that we can get inside the heart of the military and even threaten the King. She said you will take me somewhere safe afterwards. She said if we are stopped or arrested early on, I must start the process immediately.'

Jessica could not reply. Her mouth and throat dried. She nodded, throwing herself into the back of her seat, still clutching Alisha's hand wrapped with the booby trap wire. She had no intention of taking Alisha and the bomb into the dockyard. Even if she tried, they were both acting so oddly and scared, even the lax security for the Alliance would spot them.

Her mind raced. She could go along with Alisha until she found help or try to knock her out. She could wrestle the bomb from her. Perhaps she could push Alisha, with the bomb, into Portsmouth harbour from the Gosport ferry. She was using half her mental agility to prevent hyperventilating. She glanced around the carriage again, looking for inspiration and for backup.

Shamima must know how slim the odds were to get the bomb and Alisha through the gates and close to The Mary Rose, HMS Prince of Wales and the King. Perhaps Shamima would cut her losses at the estimated time of arrival and detonate the bomb using the mobile phone device. Jessica could not ignore the mobile phone might track their location, or even listen to their conversation. The only thing Jessica felt confident about: there would be no *one minute delay* from pushing the button to the bomb exploding.

The train pulled into Hilsea, a small holt to the north of the city. A woman sat in the seats across the aisle from Jessica. She sat facing the rear of the train diagonally opposite. The woman held a baby, a newborn. In tow, a toddler stood next to her. Looking slightly harassed, the woman glanced at Alisha, still rocking, and then at Jessica. The recognition was mutual and instantaneous. Alisha muttered *chaplain!* The woman reached for her phone.

'No chaplain. That is not a good idea.'

Jessica stepped across the aisle and grabbed the phone. The chaplain's eyes darted between the women and her own children. Jessica slipped the phone into her coat pocket.

'Jessica Taylor.' The chaplain pulled her baby close into her chest. 'Please Jess, they are just babies.'

'What? I will not hurt you, obviously.'

Two railway security officers entered from the second-class carriage. They stopped to check tickets of an older couple, fumbling with their phones for their senior's rail cards. Jessica switched her gaze between chaplain and Alisha, both stretching to stare at the officers.

'Chaplain, you need to trust me. Please trust me. We have a serious situation here and you must trust me to mitigate the risk.'

The chaplain now flicked her stare between her children, Jessica, Alisha, and the officers. Jessica continued speaking quietly, but urgently.

'Chaplain, please. Keep calm and stay quiet. We are all going to walk away from this. Don't put your children at risk. Trust me.'

Chaplain diverted her attention to Alisha. A few of the remaining travellers stood or stretched their necks to view the commotion. Alisha now prayed at full voice. She held the switch, her thumb firmly against the button. The security officers abandoned the elderly passengers and marched purposely along the carriage towards the three women.

'Jess! They know. Shamima told me to start the process if we get caught.'

'No Alisha, not yet! Jessica screamed. 'Out! Everyone out! She has a bomb.' The train clanked along the tracks, leaving the station. 'Move! Fucking move!'

Jessica reached for Alisha's wrist and the switch. Alisha twisted away from Jessica, folding herself into the foot space between the rows of seats.

The chaplain stood, rushing towards the rear connecting door. Other passengers blocked her way, her toddler ran in the opposite direction. Jessica scooped up the little boy and barged the chaplain ahead of her into the tight throng of people leaving the carriage. The security officers stepped into the seating to clear the way for the exiting passengers. One officer spoke into his radio as the second pushed past the passengers towards Alisha, trying not to restrict the aisle. An old woman blocked the aisle ahead. Jessica raised her leg past the chaplain and kicked the old woman through the door and into the gap between carriages.

Chaplain stumbled and fell, her full weight crushing her baby. Jessica fell with the boy and instantly bounced back onto her feet, dragging the chaplain onto her knees. In the scrum, chaplain brought the boy in front of her as Jessica reached for the fallen baby.

Chapter Thirteen

The sound of the explosion was greater than anything Jessica could have imagined. Her mind jolted to the time she witnessed missiles launch from an aircraft carrier, but this noise was infinitely greater. She felt an immense pressure collapsing her body and a heavy hammer blow to her back. A moment later followed a negative pressure, causing her cheeks and chest cavity to balloon. Shrapnel and debris punctured her body as she slammed into the bulkhead adjacent to the open connecting door.

Her surroundings muted; ears ringing. Dust filled her eyes, but she could see swirls of contrast through the dust. Her hearing was now damaged, she could only hear noises as if through water. She could not move.

Her pain was intense. Sharp pain pulsed down her neck, back, and limbs. She imagined her brain full of needles. The dust settled a little to reveal a new, grey world. She saw two booted feet in front of her. At first, she thought she must have landed on her bottom, legs extended into the sitting position. She wondered if she might have come out wearing one of her own boots and one of Alisha's. Then she realised the second severed leg was not her own.

Trying to move her head brought unbearable pain to her neck and back, but she dropped her eyes to her lap. The baby was awake. Too young to find a point of focus, her dust coated eyes rolled around indiscriminately. Her eyes were like blue gel. Jessica smiled.

A huge glass shard separated the baby from Jessica, seemingly puncturing them both. Time dragged. Jessica concentrated hard and solely on not moving the baby or her own body to further injure the baby.

The minutes passed like hours.

'Hi. You will be ok. Try not to move. Can you speak?'

'Yeah.' Jessica gurgled.

'Are you in pain?'

'Take the baby.'

'Ok. Can you let go?'

'No.'

'Ok. I am going to prise your fingers open. This might hurt.'

As the firefighter straightened each finger, pain coursed through Jessica's arm. She heard herself groan as if from outside her own body.

'Good girl. Look at that, not a scratch on the baby. You did well there. Your baby?'

'No.'

'Your name?'

'Jess.'

'I am just plain Jane. I will be your firefighter for today. Overall, what is your pain, from one to ten?'

'Million.'

'Seriously?'

'Yeah.'

'Two secs. I can sort that. You are a bit caught up. You have done the splits through the doorway. Can you move your fingers or toes?'

'Tell them both I am really sorry.'

'Tell who, Jess?'

'Jace. Tell Jace I love him.'

Jessica blacked out.

Chapter Fourteen

Jason looked around the sea of faces. One thing he did not do, was public speaking. Jessica promised, once their wedding was over, she would not make him speak publicly again until they renewed their vows as pensioners. The people he did not know personally, he guessed by where they sat or stood in groups. Amara, Jessica's best friend and colleague, sat with her wife, Willow. But other people Jason assumed were colleagues stood with faces he recognised, including Stacy and Trish. His gaze settled on Onslow, a colleague and once lover of Jessica's. He returned Jason's smile before dropping his gaze.

He saw his own friends in one part of the audience. Dawn and Sid both gave him the thumbs-up signal. He scooted over family from both sides. He had invited Priti, but she declined, feeling unnecessarily self-conscious. A chaplain sat, complete with dog collar, her husband, and two children: the baby nursing contentedly. He saw Chris, another ex of Jessica's who he met during covid lockdown. He continued along the row of in-laws and his own brother. Jessica's nieces sat separated for squabbling. Sat between them, finally, was the face he needed to see before he would find the courage to speak. Jessica beamed back, holding a niece's hand in each of her own.

People coughed and fidgeted. Jessica nodded. Jason cleared his throat.

'Thank you all. I know most of you. We all know Jess.' Jason gestured to where Jessica sat between the nieces. 'I checked the dictionary this morning. Apparently, Jessica means gorgeous and brave.' There was a smattering of nervous laughter. 'And reckless.' More laughter. When Jessica's brother-in-law added *you can say that again*, there was a small round of applause. Jessica blushed, bringing the children's hands in her own, to hide her face.

'She is one hell of a firecracker, and not always in a good way. She reacts and overreacts to every situation in which she finds herself. But she is good. She is a good person. She is a better person than me. When the chips are down, you want Jessica on your side. She even has that blasted medal from Turkey!'

The audience now roared with laughter. Each had their own understanding of the *medal*, depending on Jessica's mood and alcohol consumption when telling the story. Jessica threw back her head and laughed along at herself.

'She is the best lover, wife, friend, and soul in the world. Nobody, anywhere, none of you, are as lucky as I am to have been able to call Jessica *my own*.'

Jason froze again. He had more to say, but the courage had left him. He glanced sheepishly at Jessica, who returned a congratulatory and proud grin. The chaplain rose to her feet, still holding the nursing baby to her breast, and managed the faintest clapping to the back of her hand. Sid picked up the applause and, within a moment, the entire audience turned into a standing ovation.

Jason walked to Jessica; arms extended. The children both stood, awkwardly taking a hand each. Jason sobbed as his brother joined him, easing Jason into the empty seat between the children.

Their first wedding dance song, Light My Fire by the Doors, played over the speakers as the coffin disappeared behind the closing curtains.

Chapter Fifteen

'I will start. My name is Helen Lawrence. I hold the rank of Police Constable attached to the coroner's office. I collate information for the coroner and submit evidence with my report to the court. It is unusual, but not without precedence, to hold a pre-court meeting to discuss my report. Obviously, I cannot pre-empt any future decision of the court. Let's scoot around the room.'

The attendees introduced themselves. Jason asked for Amara to attend in support – she was calmer than Jason and quick-witted. The investigating Detective Inspector and Detective Sergeant introduced themselves. As did Detective Constable Dolly Williamson.

'Before we start, I wish to extend my condolences to you, Mr Taylor, for the tragic loss of your wife, Jessica. I offer condolences on behalf of myself, Hampshire Police, and the court. May I suggest we hold a moment's silence?' One minute later, her phone softly chimed. She cleared her throat. 'This is a complex report for a complex and tragic case in which a young woman lost her life. I have prepared a summary of some of the more salient points from my report. I can further expand on these points or try to answer questions you may have. Nothing said today will influence my report, but items may come to light which you may raise or dispute in court.

'Mrs Taylor was under investigation for a serious assault on yourself, Mr Taylor, and a family friend Priti Khan.' Helen nodded towards the investigating detectives, before continuing. 'That investigation is now complete. In consultation with the alleged victims of that assault, the Crown Prosecution Service, and Special Branch, the agencies agree it is in the public interest to close the case. Mrs Taylor has no criminal record, and the original allegation is not held on file. Understood?'

Amara and all the professionals nodded agreement, as Jason stared ahead at the table.

'I mention Special Branch, because there was an involvement with Mrs Taylor prior to her death. DC Williamson, can you expand, please?'

DC Dolly cleared his throat. 'Among other areas, Special Branch is involved in counterterrorism, along with military intelligence. I am attached to Special Branch and had a chance meeting with Mrs Taylor on the day she was arrested.'

'A chance meeting, DC Williamson?' Amara spoke.

'May I interject? In my report to the coroner,' Helen continued, 'I have advised the court that Special Branch and an individual officer are under investigation by the Constabulary as requested by the magistrate. The Constabulary, or indeed the coroner, may refer the case to the Independent Police Complaints Commission. DC Williams?'

'All I can say is, at that meeting with Mrs Taylor, we discussed the possibility Mrs Taylor might stay close to a suspected terrorist being held in the same prison. She agreed to have a tracking chip implanted under her skin. We believed that individual was planning criminal activity and a terrorist event. Shamima is that person. We suspect she authorised a prison escape using a criminal gang, and a subsequent terrorist attack in the Portsmouth area. We have made some further arrests, some subsequent to Mrs Taylor's death. Shamima and others are still at large. Mrs Taylor's brave actions are pivotal to those arrests, thwarting the full, planned terrorist attack. The contacts she made and places she visited are also pivotal to our ongoing investigations. Many individuals, and the people of Portsmouth city, can sleep easier because of Jessica Taylor.'

'How did she die? Exactly how?' Jason whispered.

Helen cleared her throat. 'Mrs Taylor was on a train to Portsmouth Harbour when her travel companion detonated an explosive device. From the actions of Mrs Taylor immediately prior to the explosion, and following a brief conversation she had with the prison chaplain in a chance meeting, I will advise the coroner to consider Mrs Taylor was bravely trying to prevent and then mitigate the effects of the explosion. The suspected bomber was also killed in the explosion. Several others sustained life changing injuries and a railway security officer remains in hospital. Evidence suggests, as terrible as the attack was, Mrs Taylor prevented further loss of life and injury by the actions she took.'

'I said, how did she die!'

'Mrs Taylor used her body to shield a baby and a small child from the blast. As a result, she suffered multiple injuries. Specifically, Mrs Taylor suffered a large triangular shard of glass, from a control panel, entering her back. It severed her spine, puncturing one lung, and protruded from the front of her torso. The injuries proved catastrophic.'

'Did she die quickly? Was she in pain?'

Helen studied her own report, of which she knew every word, in an effort to compose herself.

'The initial injury to her spine is likely to have caused immediate paralysis. In a heroic effort, Mrs Taylor remained conscious for long enough to cradle safely the baby until help arrived. Mrs Taylor remained conscious for some time.' Helen scanned her report again, swallowing hard. 'Mrs Taylor remained conscious for twenty-six minutes, protecting the baby. She was pronounced dead on arrival at the hospital forty-two minutes later. She probably actually died from her injuries, on losing consciousness at the twenty-six-minute point.'

Jason spoke in a barely audible growl. 'This is very hard for me. Please do not make me repeat myself.'

Helen swallowed several times and blew her nose, fighting back tears. 'It is likely Mrs Taylor was in considerable pain throughout the twenty-six minutes she fought to stay alive and keep the baby safe.'

'Was she alone at the end?'

'Firefighter Jane held Mrs Taylor's hand as she lost consciousness. She spoke a few words.'

'Jess spoke? To the firefighter?'

Helen nodded. 'To the best of firefighter Jane's recollection, Mrs Taylor answered to say she could not move and was in considerable pain. She told Jane to take the baby from her. She asked Jane to *tell you both she was sorry*. Her last words were *Jace. Tell Jace I love him*.